GOLDSTRIKE

ALSO BY MATT WHYMAN

Icecore

GOLDSTRIKE

A THRILLER

MATT WHYMAN

Atheneum Books for Young Readers
New York London Toronto Sydney

ATHENEUM BOOKS FOR YOUNG READERS

An imprint of Simon & Schuster Children's Publishing Division

1230 Avenue of the Americas, New York, New York 10020

Originally published in Great Britain in 2009 by Simon & Schuster UK Ltd

ATHENEUM BOOKS FOR YOUNG READERS is a registered trademark of Simon & Schuster, Inc.

For information about special discounts for bulk purchases, please contact Simon & Schuster Special Sales at 1-866-506-1949 or business@simonandschuster.com.

The Simon & Schuster Speakers Bureau can bring authors to your live event. For more information or to book an event, contact the Simon & Schuster Speakers Bureau at 1-866-248-3049 or visit our website at www.simonspeakers.com.

Also available in an Atheneum Books for Young Readers hardcover edition.

Book design by Paul Weil

The text for this book is set in Garamond.

Manufactured in the United States of America

First Atheneum Books for Young Readers paperback edition February 2011

10 9 8 7 6 5 4 3 2 1

The Library of Congress has cataloged the hardcover edition as follows:

Whyman, Matt.

Goldstrike : a thriller / Matt Whyman. —1st ed.

p. cm.

Summary: After escaping Camp Twilight, eighteen-year-old Carl Hobbes and Beth, his girlfriend, begin a new life in London, England, where he attempts to program Sphinx Cargo's highly intelligent supercomputer to help protect them from the CIA and assassins.

ISBN 978-1-4169-9510-4 (hc)

[1. Fugitives from justice—Fiction. 2. Computer hackers—Fiction. 3. Supercomputers—Fiction. 4. Assassins—Fiction. 5. United States. Central Intelligence Agency—Fiction. 6. London (England)—Fiction. 7. England—Fiction.] I. Title.

PZ7.W623Gol 2010

[Fic]—dc22

2009017830

ISBN 978-1-4169-9511-1 (pbk)

To all those readers who kept asking

what happened to Hobbes

ACKNOWLEDGMENTS

I should like to thank my editor, Venetia Gosling, for her long-standing support, fine humor, and expertise, as well as the entire team at Simon & Schuster. I'm also very grateful to Philippa Milnes-Smith and Ayesha Mobin for keeping the wolves at bay.

Finally, to my family for everything else.

OLD CITY, SANA'A, REPUBLIC OF YEMEN, THE MIDDLE EAST

IN BLACK SUITS AND DARK GLASSES, THE THREE MEN STAND OUT AMONG the throng. Even without ties, their top buttons undone at the throat, they couldn't look more Western if they tried. Here, just inside the gates to this ancient heart of the capital, known as Bab al-Yemen, the people are dressed in customary robes, shawls, and sandals.

The women are veiled, while the men sport decorative daggers, or *jambia*, around their waists, as is the local custom.

"Hey, Americans!" A group of kids sitting on a step are the first to remark on the trio. Only one might speak a little English, but some others join in by firing imaginary pistols.

The three men move with a purpose, crossing the square toward the ornate basalt buildings and labyrinth of winding alleyways. They remain entirely unconcerned by the fact that their presence is causing heads to turn. Nor do they pause to take in the stalls selling boiled eggs, spices, and flatbread. The man who leads

1

the way, a heavyset individual who is sweating noticeably, touches a finger to a tiny microphone clipped to his collar.

"Target sighted," he reports. "We have a visual."

Minutes earlier, just outside the gates, the young man they're following had climbed out of a cab. Within this walled quarter, most of the passages are just too narrow for anything but motorbikes and carts. He'd paid the driver, neglecting to tip as he looked around, before heading off on foot. The three men had waited for him to reach the main square before breaking their cover. Coming from different directions, they had converged in his wake without a word.

Their target moves at a brisk pace. He avoids all eye contact with market traders. Just keeps his head down. Even begins to weave around those in his path. To the men now closing the gap, this is no cause for alarm. Dressed in jeans and a casual shirt, with a canvas bag slung over one shoulder, this is one outsider who's as conspicuous as they are. Most probably he's bought into the fear that being in the open like this is an invitation to opportunist kidnappers. As it is, the people he's actually come so far to avoid are just seconds behind him. Biding time before they pounce.

The alley leads toward the central souk, a bustling market under slanting sheets to shade it from the sun. From dawn to dusk, this is where jewelry, sandals, carpets, and leather goods are made and sold. Their target ducks left before he reaches it. This surprises the men. Immediately they rush for the corner. From there, they spot him passing a whitewashed mosque. He's moving a little faster now, on the cusp of breaking into a jog. Such is his pace that it's tough for the trio to keep up without betraying their intention. It's also hard to know if it means he's onto them. Still, there's no way now that they can lose him. After so long on the run, Carl Hobbes cannot be allowed to slip away.

Dark, barren mountains surround Sana'a, a city spiked by teetering minarets. Minutes from now, the call to prayer will issue from them all, and the sound will thunder far and wide. By then, if the operation goes according to plan, these CIA operatives will at last have their prize.

Unusually, they carry only sidearms. An indication, perhaps, that they're expecting no trouble. Online, things were very different. As a hacker, the individual in their sights posed a threat to global stability. For months intelligence had been warning that Hobbes could take down stock markets with a keystroke. The talk that he might hold America's air traffic control network for ransom had yet to be proven, but those guys were rattled. As for the military, every system administrator had been warned to expect a strike at any moment. And, when it came, so they said, it would be the virtual equivalent of a shock-and-awe campaign.

Away from computers and phone lines, however, the threat diminished considerably. As the agents on his tail can see for

3

themselves, Hobbes is just some eighteen-year-old upstart. A troublemaker at large who'd been flashing up randomly all over their global radar like some damn UFO. Of course, it was only a matter of time before he made the mistake that brought them here. When you're this high on America's Most Wanted list, there's no place on the planet where it's safe to use your real name. Not even here, on the southernmost tip of the Arabian Peninsula. You couldn't even whisper it without needles tweaking into the red.

For whatever reason Hobbes had given away his location, checking into a hotel as himself some days earlier. It's clear to the three agents that he's on full alert right now. All it takes is a glance over his shoulder, as if to confirm something he's sensed, and suddenly he's tearing through the dust.

The men behind him miss a beat in their scramble to respond. With people milling around outside the mosque, they're forced to go wide as they give chase.

"He's spooked!" The operative with the radio contact draws his weapon as he runs. "We are good to go!"

Having studied the maps, these guys know their target could melt away at any moment. With so many blind corners, converging passages, courtyards, and corrals, it's possible for him to vanish at the first opportunity. But instead of stealing the advantage, the idiot reacts like some startled rooster and simply bowls directly for his hotel.

A guard sits in a plastic chair outside the entrance. He holds a rifle halfheartedly across his lap. Still, he makes no move to intervene when the three men hurriedly enter the building. Having witnessed the boy rush inside a moment ago, some young British visitor he's seen around the last few days, it's clear they're here for him. The handguns in their possession also persuade him to remain where he is. The guard might be here to safeguard anyone staying inside, but he's merely window decoration. In this region, you take care of your own security measures. Besides, these three look like they're here to combat any threat.

"Gentlemen?" The woman behind the reception desk speaks with a classroom English accent. She is robed, with her veil folded back, revealing carefully made-up eyes. Most striking of all is her cool composure in the face of such a dramatic arrival. The three men have just crashed inside the lobby. They're panting heavily. Positioned in a fan formation. Handguns tipped upward.

"Carl?" one of the agents calls out. "It's over, Hobbes! Do the right thing!"

"Where did he go?" The heavyset man snaps out his identification wallet.

The receptionist takes one look and appears to freeze. "C'mon, lady!" he adds fractiously. "The kid who just ran in here . . . Talk to me!"

Without taking her eyes off the men, she gestures at the elevator. "He went to his room."

"301, right?" He glances at his colleagues, still panting but with a hint of jubilation now. "No need to tell him we're here."

The men cut to the elevator door. When it opens, the receptionist watches them hurriedly gather inside. As soon as the door closes, she punches the room number into the booking system. What appears on the monitor leaves her looking baffled. She turns and unlocks a cabinet drawer. From a hanging file, she pulls out photocopies of the passport details for every guest who has checked in. That many of the rooms are vacant just reflects the threat level here in a hotel once popular with Westerners. It also means the few people in residence are no strangers to her. The receptionist begins to leaf through the wad, searching for the name on the screen, before grabbing the phone to call the duty manager.

Hobbes. Carl Hobbes. That's what she had heard the man call out when they burst in here. It just isn't the name she remembers for the young guy they're after. He'd checked in as James Valentine, and the paperwork in her hand confirms this. What's weird is that the online booking system is showing the name she'd heard just now. She mutters to herself, urging the duty manager to pick up. Whoever he was, the guest in question had been notably demanding since he showed up.

On his arrival, two days earlier, she'd assumed at first he was either one of those spoiled Western rich kids—an ambassador's son, perhaps—or just edgy about his safety so far from home and not expressing it well. As the day wore on, and the calls to reception mounted, she had marked him down as someone who simply needed to learn some manners. First the room service meal he'd ordered hadn't come with ketchup. Then came a complaint about the quality of the television picture. She recalls now that he's here for some university cultural exchange program. Whatever his role in that, his behavior meant she remembers him. One thing is for sure, however. Carl Hobbes is *definitely* not the name he gave when he checked in. She drums her nails on the keyboard's plastic housing, staring at the monitor. Finally, when the voice of her duty manager does come through, she is entirely distracted by a change on the screen.

"Wait a minute . . . *how?*"

Her hand is nowhere near the mouse, and yet the cursor has just drifted into the name field. It's as if some ghost spirit has seized control of her screen. An invisible presence who begins to delete every letter, working back through Hobbes and then Carl. A moment later the name is replaced by that of the high-maintenance young man three floors up. The one currently cowering as the door to his room is kicked down. Finally a simple instruction appears. It lasts only as long as it takes for the receptionist to draw a breath in shock, and then it is gone:

shhhhh ;-)

CASINO OCEANIA, MONTEVIDEO, URUGUAY
SIXTEEN DAYS LATER

THE YOUNG MAN HAD MONEY TO BURN. THAT MUCH WAS CLEAR TO the casino staff, the card dealers, and the cashier behind the bulletproof glass. He had shown up late on Tuesday, played a couple of unremarkable hands, and then let roll the kind of sums you'd expect from a Russian oil baron.

At times he got lucky, but mostly it went the dealer's way. Throughout the ups and all the downs, however, he continued quietly to attract attention. Right now, by his side at the crowded poker table sits a dark-haired woman. Perched on a high stool under a light, she's wearing a red cocktail dress that reveals a slender back. Up on the balcony, a member of the security team is watching the pair impassively, as are two of his colleagues via the monitors in the basement. Another figure in the basement stands behind them, watching the same screen. But he does not work for the casino.

The special agent is here on a tip-off from the cashier, who is on his payroll.

The CIA had eyes and ears like this all over the world. Reports of individuals who bore a vague resemblance to Hobbes's description came in every day. But so had the patient database from the hard drive of an Estonian plastic surgeon, one who specialized in underworld makeovers. With Hobbes's name on the list, along with details of extensive facial reconstruction work, it meant any likeness had to be treated with some caution. Certainly the individual in the frame here shares a passing resemblance in terms of his slim build and relative youth. He had also raised suspicions by signing into a nearby hotel under a name that didn't match the one on his credit card—but even that wasn't what drew the agent.

Nor was it the money.

Hobbes undoubtedly had access to huge funds. Given his role in tapping into the security system at the Fort Knox gold bullion depository, he had to be one flush hacker. You didn't just open up the vault for your accomplice without reward. Even though the kid hadn't confessed to stashing some of that haul for himself, only a fool would've passed on every single bar. At the detainment camp, following his capture, Hobbes's interrogators had worked on breaking him down. With more time, confirmation would've come that the entire operation had been carried out to fund terror cells.

As it turned out, the relationship between the hacker and his handlers had come to an abrupt and unexpected end.

Just like his colleagues, this special agent regarded the uprising among the detainees and the subsequent breakout as a sorry mess. State secrets had a habit of going public, after all, which made the recapture of a central player like Hobbes all the more pressing. Even so, they couldn't go chasing after every young playboy who threw his wealth around, especially as many used alternative names to keep the press at bay.

What scrambled the agent into action here was solid proof that Hobbes had surfaced at last.

It came down to a fingerprint. Picked up from one of the many hundred-dollar bills that had left the suspect's money clip, it matched the hacker's 100 percent.

Observing the monitor still, the agent opens the channel on his walkie-talkie.

"Ruthie, ask what he likes best about Uruguay. I'm curious, is all."

On the screen, as if in response, the woman with the cocktail drink curls a strand of hair behind one ear and then converses with the young man. At the same time, the speaker under the monitor confirms that she's just put the question to him.

"I like that nobody knows who I am," the young man can be

heard to say. *"In London I can't leave my apartment without thinking I'll be recognized. It's the same in Monaco, too."*

"Smooth," the agent mutters, and then addresses the two men before him. "Can you believe he told her he's a racecar driver? Man, we could all learn something from him. Just look at the way she's resting her hand on his knee now! Either she's play-acting real well, or the lines he's spinning really are working." He chuckles to himself, only for static to spit from the walkie-talkie before another voice addresses him.

"Mother two, we are in position. On your word, we can play our hand."

The agent sighs to himself, nodding now. "As much as I'd like to witness more tips on charming the chicks, you can proceed at will. And let's shake him up in the process," he adds, as an afterthought. "Yeah, why not? Anyone who thinks their luck is in with Ruthie needs to be cut down to size."

Clipping the walkie-talkie onto his belt, the agent buttons his jacket at the middle and watches the screen intently. As the target plays his final hand, watched closely by the CIA plant in the cocktail dress, a fine beam of light floats across the floor toward him. It climbs up his back, coming to rest on the nape of his neck, followed closely behind by another. Quietly the woman moves aside, and that's when the marksmen on the balcony command their target to freeze or receive a skullful of hot lead.

11

CIA HEADQUARTERS, FAIRFAX COUNTY, VIRGINIA, USA
FORTY MINUTES AGO

A LONG PAUSE FOLLOWS THE CONCLUSION OF THE ACTIVITY REPORT. The personnel around the table consider what they have just been told with an air of grim acceptance. More than a dozen men and women are present, some in civilian clothing, others in military uniform. Behind them, aides stand awkwardly, waiting for someone to break the silence. At the top end of the table, in front of the electronic whiteboard with the blowup of the fingerprint data file on it, the intelligence officer who has just delivered the report clears his throat.

"We couldn't have known at the time," he tells them. "The computer database confirmed that the prints were identical for every marker. It was a perfect match for Hobbes."

The woman at the far end listens intently. She's dressed in a sober three-piece suit offset by an ornate brooch. This is Pamela Boyers, assistant to the president for national security affairs, and the most senior individual present. She sits with her hands clasped on the table and a look of sheer disbelief on her face.

"And yet this turns out not to be the case, correct?"

"So it seems, ma'am."

"Because someone hacked into the database and manipulated the code to set up this gentleman." She pauses there, refers to her notes, and looks back, shaking her head.

"Our tech guys are onto it now. Their initial conclusion is that the perpetrator altered the program so that any search on the suspect's fingerprint would've returned the data file for Carl Hobbes. Rather than compare the images, this one was *copied* automatically to Hobbes's file, effectively overwriting the print we had for him and providing the exact match."

Pamela Boyers presses her hands into a steeple. "Aside from the embarrassment caused to the president by so dramatically apprehending a popular British sportsman, do we have a backup of the Carl Hobbes data file?"

The intelligence officer presses his lips together. He then shuts down the electronic whiteboard. "We have his other digits, ma'am."

For a moment, with her head bowed, Ms. Boyers looks as if she is praying. "Can we assume Carl Hobbes himself perpetrated this attack?"

"We traced the user's IP address. It took us to a cybercafé in Singapore. Our people over there paid a visit. The place was closed when the incursion onto our network took place. Server records show that every computer terminal was switched off. It can only mean the hacker used the server as a stepping-stone. So far we've traced back through twelve in the chain, at random points around the globe, but to be frank, ma'am, he could've run a program to take him through thousands."

With a sigh, Boyers sits back in her chair. "The fact that he's found his way onto our system tells me it must be Hobbes."

"Without a doubt, he knows how to exploit the weak points," replies the intelligence officer.

"So shall we make an educated guess that he was behind last week's false lead to the Middle East?"

The intelligence officer reaches for the knot of his tie. "We found a remote view program on the hotel's desktop. It's what allowed Hobbes to take it over and mess with the guest records."

"And how did this program find its way onto the desktop?" asks Boyers.

"He'd e-mailed it to one of the managers a few days earlier, having hijacked an e-mail address belonging to the man's brother. It was masked as a family wedding picture, so he was bound to open it up."

Boyers considers this for a moment. "Presumably Hobbes covered his tracks by using the stepping-stone technique you outlined earlier."

The intelligence officer confirms this with a nod.

"He just doesn't slip up. But we will get him. No hacker is totally invisible. There has to be a trail, no matter how buried it may be."

"Nevertheless, this is the seventh time since his escape that we have been sent on a wild-goose chase to some random part of the world." Boyers sounds a little irritated all of a sudden. "We have the resources, and yet he continues to outwit us. People, he's only just turned *eighteen* years of age! I shouldn't have to trouble myself with individual cases at this level. We have egg on our faces here."

"With respect, ma'am, we cannot be guaranteed that Hobbes is spearheading the hoaxes." The man who stops her short is sitting to her right. He's long limbed, uneasy-looking, with a shirt collar too big for his neck. Nervously, he pushes his oval spectacles to the bridge of his nose. "There is a strong possibility that he's not even *alive*." He looks around the room, as if seeking some support. Farther down the table, a member of the military shuffles his papers. "We know the detainee who was with Hobbes perished in their bid to get away. In temperatures of minus seventeen, the coroner estimated that Beth Nelson died from hypothermia within an hour of the breakout." He pauses there to locate a page in the dossier before him. What he finds causes him to tighten his lips. "The photographs taken at the scene suggest that Hobbes had laid her to rest in the snow. The girl was his accomplice in the Fort Knox raid, so you can imagine he felt the loss hard. As he faced another hundred and twenty-two kilometers of treacherous wilderness before hitting the nearest outpost, it's fair to argue that he couldn't have gotten much farther. In those conditions, he would've just lost the will to live."

"And yet only one body was recovered," Boyers notes.

"Camp Twilight was located on Svalbard," he reminds everyone. "It's a cruel, storm-blown cluster of islands in the Arctic Ocean. In terms of the elements, this is one hostile place. We're talking everything from glacial fjords to wild, rugged mountains. Hobbes's corpse could be out there, ma'am, but combing that landscape is just unrealistic. Even if we found a way to cover the terrain comprehensively, chances are wolves have claimed every bone by now."

Pamela Boyers hears him out and then sits back in her chair.

"Maybe he just flew out," she says with a shrug. The silence that follows her suggestion seems to thicken in the air. Boyers lets it hang there for a moment longer. "The boy knows how to manipulate security systems, right? With emergency personnel drafted in to deal with the aftermath, it's fair to say Camp Twilight was in a state of chaos. Who's to say he didn't slip back undercover and turn that to his advantage?"

The man from the military shakes his head. "It would be unthinkable."

"But not impossible," she replies, cutting him dead. With a sigh, she addresses the table once more. "How many people take the view that Hobbes is deceased?"

Hesitantly, the bespectacled individual who had voiced his doubts raises his hand.

His military counterpart closes his dossier. He shakes his head, clearly rankled still by Boyers's suggestion. "It had to be he took his chances in the wild."

Visibly exasperated, the man across from him lowers his hand. "But Hobbes would've *known* that such an escape bid was suicide. It was spelled out to every new arrival. The detainment camp was *deliberately* sited on such a remote outpost as a deterrent to those on the inside, as much as anyone hoping to bust them out."

"Which is precisely what happened," Ms. Boyers cuts in. "It might be classified information, but the uprising at Camp Twilight is not something we can brush under the carpet. As I'm well aware, Beth Nelson wasn't the only individual to perish out there. Too many people lost their lives on both sides. If it ever leaks that a military detainee is on the run, or if Carl himself chooses to go public, all hell will break loose in the media. The fact that he can breeze in and out of computer systems, including our own, makes this a matter of the utmost urgency. Not only do we have no idea where he is in the world, it appears that he knows *exactly* what our movements are in our efforts to bring him to justice. Every time our system is compromised, we take measures to ensure it never happens again, and he just finds another way in. Do any of you *realize* how useful his abilities could be to the terror organizations?"

"That's one thing we don't have to concern ourselves with." The man from the military looks almost relieved that she has raised this point. "The chatter we've picked up suggests that Al-Qaeda holds Hobbes personally responsible for the deaths of some of their key figures during the uprising at Camp Twilight. It's not just us after him, ma'am. The only difference is, they want him terminated."

"That hardly puts us *close* to being on the same side, Commander, though it may go some way to explaining why he has gone to ground." As Boyers speaks, an aide steps forward and whispers in her ear. She nods and gathers her papers, preparing to leave. "Tell me this. What will it take to bring Hobbes into custody . . . assuming he *is* alive?" she adds pointedly.

"Our finest people are on it," the military man tells her.

"Which is clearly not good enough," she replies. "Is there a price on his head? Perhaps we should enlist some external help to track him down."

The suggestion is met with an uncomfortable murmuring.

"Ma'am, the problem with that is the bounty hunters." This is the intelligence agent who had delivered the report. "Often they don't operate within the law."

"And yet they get the job done. So, what are we looking at

to capture him? Al-Qaeda might be out for retribution, but we could certainly use him on our side. Put a figure on it, gentlemen. I don't care how we net the boy, so long as he's still breathing. C'mon, a million bucks?"

"Try ten."

The assistant to the president for national security affairs rises from her seat.

"Make it twenty. Whatever it takes, I want Carl Hobbes *offline*."

1

SPHINX CARGO, HEATHROW AIRPORT INDUSTRIAL ESTATE, ENGLAND
RIGHT NOW

THIS IS NOT A GOOD TIME FOR A JOB INTERVIEW. IT'S HARD TO FEEL AT your best when soaked to the skin. The rain started falling on the bus ride here. By the time we reached my stop, I had stepped out into a deluge.

As I stand outside the main door, waiting to be buzzed in, I just know I should've checked the forecast. My interviewer is bound to take one look at me and question my ability to plan ahead. It wouldn't have taken much foresight to bring an umbrella or waterproof coat. I feel self-conscious enough as it is without the security camera trained on me. If anyone is behind it right now, it must look to them as if I've swum here.

"Okay, come on through."

I hear the locking mechanism retract and give the door a

push. It doesn't budge. I try again. The third time, the voice through the intercom returns.

"Pull the door, sir. Pull it to open."

Whatever the weather, any industrial park feels bleak. This one is laid out in a grid. From each road and intersection, giant warehouses can be seen set back behind staff parking lots and conifer trees in concrete planters. Some are decked out in corporate colors with logos on display at every opportunity. Others are drab and anonymous, and the one I'm visiting now is a case in point. What makes this windowless steel structure so notable is its sheer size. You could fit several soccer fields inside and have room to loft the ball high. Even so, for such a vast building there's no sense of design, style, or passion. The main entrance is the only feature at the front. The concrete crash barriers that stand sentry around it hardly make for a warm welcome. In fact, the only confirmation that I've come to the right place is the corporate nameplate beside the intercom buzzer.

Having mastered the door, I wish myself luck and step in from the rain.

What I find inside is in stark contrast to the exterior. From the glass security pod, I look out across a polished marble floor and wait for the receptionist to press the release button. She does so with a smile and a nod for me to come on through.

I exit the pod, knowing I have just been swept by a radio imager to detect for weapons or explosives.

The receptionist is standing at a desk that is dwarfed by the statue behind her. Protruding from the wall, illuminated by careful lighting, the body of a giant lion with the head of a ram looks down on this atrium area. It's so impressive that the receptionist's desk has been custom-built to fit neatly between this mythical creature's front paws.

"Welcome to Sphinx Cargo," she says as I approach the desk. It's evident she's noted that I'm utterly drenched. Courageously, I think, her smile does not slip. "Is the rain showing any sign of clearing up?"

I glance at the glass ceiling high above.

"You might want to skip eating out for lunch," I say, grinning sheepishly. "I have an appointment to see Mr. Thorn."

"Your name?"

"Carter," I say. "Finn Carter."

The receptionist consults her screen. The badge on her jacket tells me this is Sara Sinclair. I am also aware that she turns twenty-six next month and lives with her boyfriend, who loves her deeply but has some debt problems. More important to me, she uses the name of her first pet for all her passwords on their home computer.

"Mr. Thorn is just finishing with another candidate," she

says, and invites me to sign in. Instead of a visitors' book, I am presented with a touch-screen tablet. I tap out my name using the back of the pen she hands me, confirm the time of my arrival, and fill in the box with a signature that is now second nature to me. "Take a seat, sir. He'll see you shortly."

2

FORTUNATELY, MY PASSPORT HAS ESCAPED GETTING WET.

So too has my driver's license. I had kept them both in the inside pocket of my jacket. The employment agency who secured this interview had instructed me to bring them along. I had also been asked to sign a consent form that allowed Sphinx Cargo to run a police check on me. This was basically a way for a potential employer to find out whether I hid a criminal history of any kind.

I return the documents to my pocket, aware that this is one thing I don't have to worry about, and focus on presenting myself as best I can.

It's very quiet in here. Unlike the neighboring warehouses, I noted few vehicles in the parking lot outside. There is just one door into the main building itself. It's accessed from an open staircase with tempered glass steps and chrome railings, and yet nobody comes or goes. The receptionist taps away gently at her keyboard, and that is the only sound to be heard. I study the wall opposite the statue of the sphinx. It is etched with hieroglyphics. Instinctively, I try to read a line. As I begin to work out a pattern, so the peace gives way to a growing whine.

Within seconds it turns to a roar. I glance at the receptionist. She doesn't even look away from her screen. Just as the noise reaches an alarming pitch, wall-to-wall shadows sweep across the floor. Looking up through the glass ceiling, I catch sight of the belly of a huge aircraft passing overhead.

"Wow!" I declare. "That must take some getting used to."

I only remark on this because I think it would seem weird to ignore it completely. I know full well that the warehouse is located at the east end of the runway, behind the apron road. I had studied enough online maps to be familiar with every service lane and alleyway in the vicinity, should the need arise for a quick exit. On this occasion, when the receptionist finally looks across at me, I realize that I could've let it go without comment.

"I'm sorry, sir. Did you just say something?"

I twiddle my thumbs uncomfortably. "Just that you're exceptionally close to the runway here."

"Oh, you mean the plane?" she asks, as if the dwindling noise has only just come to her attention. "Sometimes they do come in a little low like that," she adds, and then pauses to consider me. "Would you like a towel or something?"

Before I can politely decline, the door at the top of the open staircase swings outward. The tail end of a conversation can be heard, after which a stocky young man is led out into the atrium by the individual I am here to see.

The candidate's name is James Murdo. He is twenty-three, with four years' experience working as a freelance bodyguard. According to the form he completed online for the employment agency, James listed his interests as keeping fit, which is evident now that I see him. His pumped frame is squeezed into a suit that is clearly on the small side. Unlike mine, however, it is quite dry. I watch the two men shake hands before he turns to leave the atrium. He nods at me on passing, not that we have ever met. He also seems quite confident, which is no surprise. On paper, he appears well qualified for the job.

I could've sabotaged his chances, of course, and also those of the three other candidates who have made it to the interview stage. Then again, I know how it feels to be the victim of an injustice. Instead, in a bid to play fair, I cooked up a résumé that would give me a fighting chance over the competition, if not the edge.

"Finn Carter?" At once I am on my feet and reaching for the outstretched hand of Sphinx Cargo's security director. "Willard Thorn." Like many of this American company's senior staff, Thorn has been brought in from across the water. With cinnamon skin and an easy smile, he looks like a man who could also handle their media relations. "I guess you heard the jet come over," he says, grinning now. "Scared the bejesus out of me the first time. Nowadays it reminds me that there is a world outside this baby. It's kinda reassuring."

Thorn looks me straight in the eye when he says all this. I know he's noted the sorry state of my suit but leaves me with no hint of being marked down for it. I warm to him immediately.

"The seven-two-sevens are the loudest," I tell him, and now my smile outshines his own. "My flat is under the flight path as well."

Willard Thorn nods approvingly and then invites me to cross the atrium floor with him. "So, this could be a home away from home for you?"

"I certainly hope so," I reply, as the drone of the next incoming plane begins to grow.

3

MIDWAY UP THE GLASS STAIRS, WILLARD THORN PAUSES AND INVITES me to look around.

"Impressive, isn't she?"

"It isn't what I expected," I say, nodding in agreement. "From the outside, you'd think it was just another warehouse."

"That's precisely how our clients like it," he says. "If we attracted too much attention, it would frighten them away."

Thorn continues to lead the way. At the top, we face a steel door. There is no handle or key slot. The control panel beside it just hints at the technology I know to be wired inside. From the camera lens to the finger pad, this is state-of-the-art biometric security.

"Do I need a pass?" I ask innocently.

"You *are* the pass!" replies Thorn. "Let me show you." Turning to the panel now, he stands in front of the camera lens, rolling his shoulders as he does so. With a *bleep*, a fan of infrared light beams plays over his face. They sweep around for a moment and then form into two clusters on finding his eyes.

"Anyone can steal a PIN number," he says as each light source slowly revolves. "We know some people are prepared to steal eyeballs as well, but even that won't get you through. The system here waits for you to blink, just to prove you're alive, and that can't be faked."

As he tells me this, the beams shut off. With a beep, the door clicks outward. I find myself peering into a small, brightly lit chamber. It's fitted with grilles top and bottom.

"Another security pod?" I ask.

Thorn smiles at my assumption.

"You were dusted down for weapons and explosives at the main door. This one actually dusts *you* down. It's basically an airlock that works by washing out the air with a purified feed from her tanks. We don't want any contamination risk, as I'm sure you'll appreciate. But before we step inside I need you to step up to the camera and look directly into the lens."

I take his place in front of the console. "What happens if someone tries to get in without authorization?" I ask as he punches in what must be a guest code on the keypad.

"The device is programmed to blind."

I look at him, a little lost for words, only for that grin to ease across his face.

"I'm kidding," he declares. "If you're not authorized, you don't get in. It's as simple as that. Now, smile for the camera."

The light beams play over my face.

"Is this for the record?" I ask, as the device finds my eyes.

"That's correct. As is the sampling of your voice that occurred when you signed in at reception." With the scan complete, he invites me to look down at the receptionist's desk. From this angle, we have a clear view of her monitor. I see a jagged graph blown up in a window. "Finn, this building knows more about your identity than your own mother right now."

As the receptionist's fingers dart over the keyboard, the image then shrinks to fit beside my signature and the retinal scan I have just provided. Underneath, strings of text begin to upload. It might be too far away for me to read, but I am sure every electronic stone on the Internet is currently being turned to build a profile of me. Despite the background checks and these steps to ensure that nobody can attempt to access the building pretending to be me, I know the final step will not be taken by computer. As I look back to Willard Thorn, I find him considering me straight on.

"I brought my passport," I tell him, fishing in my pocket now. "And my driver's license."

The security director takes the documents. He flips open the passport and compares me to the picture inside. "For all the technological precautions," he says, "I provide the final clearance." He falls quiet there, contemplating me now, and then switches his attention to my license. I want to swallow, but fight the urge. Thorn holds back on a smile. I am sure he has noticed. "You're probably thinking it would be easier getting through a customs checkpoint," he continues, "and in many ways, you'd be right. Once I'm through with you here, you'll be stepping into territory that is effectively off-limits to the outside world. Now, you might think I'm taking a risk by inviting candidates into such an environment, but I'll level with you here. There is no way that anyone can compromise this system. It has to be that way, as I'm sure you'll appreciate in a moment."

"I'm ready," I say, smiling when he returns my documents.

"Be my guest," replies Thorn, and invites me to step inside the airlock.

4

IT ISN'T JUST PASSENGERS WHO PASS THROUGH A MAJOR INTER-national airport. All kinds of cargo are flown in and out, from perishable goods to machine parts, critical medicines, live animals, and even dead bodies. It means specialist storage and handling facilities can always be found nearby.

In particular, when it comes to transporting items of great value, clients need to be assured that their goods are placed in very safe hands indeed.

Stepping onto the gantry walkway on the other side of the airlock, I get my first sense of just why Sphinx Cargo is rated as the most secure, elite, and exclusive storage facility on earth. I know it must hold paintings with conservation concerns because the lighting is set at a very low level and dehumidifiers can be heard humming. Even so, when my surroundings take shape through the carefully controlled gloom, I have to struggle to stop my jaw from falling.

"This is astonishing," I say under my breath. "It's like a treasure trove!"

"We think of it more as a pharaoh's tomb," Thorn comments from behind. "It fits the company image."

All around this cavernous space, stacked in block after block of pallet racks, I find myself taking in priceless items of every description. I'm looking at everything from grand vases and bronze sculptures to Islamic ceramics and carefully stacked canvases. Most immediately, I set eyes on several consignments of the precious metal that sent me to hell and back. There it is, glittering defiantly.

"Shouldn't some of this stuff be packed in boxes?" I ask, anxious not to focus on the gold bullion bars down there.

"Any other freight storage facility would be guilty of negligence for not doing so," Thorn tells me. "In here, the environment is so precisely manipulated that it simply isn't necessary. The air is entirely free from dust, bacteria, and moisture, and the light is ultraviolet free. All the elements that might otherwise mean some items demand individual care we've just removed from the equation. Critically, the air is low on the one thing that will leave you short of breath if you spend too long on this walkway." As he says this, I realize that the air is notably thin in here. "The oxygen supply is purposely restricted to help preserve some of the older paintings, and especially any parchment papers. We do it by pumping in a little nitrogen. We have to be careful, of course. Anything over eighty percent could kill in a short space of time and without any symptoms. That's why striking the right balance is a fine art in itself," he jokes. "It's no laughing matter when you begin to feel faint, so let's keep moving."

The walkway spans the length of the building. It's suspended from a cradle of fine steel wires. With subtle floor lights studding each side, and a pool of darkness below, we could be floating on air. I certainly feel a little giddiness but assume this is because of the reduced oxygen setup. It's then I detect the slightest rumble overhead. Compared to the last aircraft this is just a whisper, and a measure of the thickness of the building's outer shell. Constructed from reinforced steel and concrete, and tiled with solar panels to feed a backup generator, it makes me feel as if I could survive the end of the world in here.

As we advance, I note the network of overhead cranes. Several are in action. I watch a grab claw swoop away on a robotic arm, descending into the gloom as it moves, while another overtakes us with a crate harnessed underneath stamped BOSTON MUSEUM OF FINE ARTS.

"The entire operation is fully automated," Thorn tells me. "Computers don't get giddy without clean air to breathe, y'see."

"How long are things stored here?" I ask, looking up and around as I walk.

"Much depends on the red tape," replies Thorn. "When it comes to air freight, inspections have to be carried out, licenses issued, and taxes paid. It all depends on the nature of the cargo and the destination. Whatever the case, it can take time. Anything from a couple of days to several years." I turn when he says this, wondering whether he's fooling with me once more. Thorn just shrugs, as if it's out of his hands. "Sphinx was established in response to the number of bullion robberies carried out worldwide on cargo warehouses. We spotted the demand for a fail-safe system and found ourselves running at full capacity within three months. One or two items that arrived when we first opened have yet to receive a dispatch order. But hey, so long as the client keeps paying the bills, we're happy to oblige."

As we approach the far end of the walkway, Willard Thorn elects to stride ahead. We are heading toward another airlock. I can see this will take us into a closed gallery at the far end. Supported on three giant steel columns, the gallery runs from one side of the building to the other and overlooks the entire space. Through the darkened windows in the center, I glimpse blinking lights from within a section of a computer framework. This time I make no comment.

I am already well aware that this is the control hub for Sphinx Cargo.

Naturally, as a candidate for a job here, Thorn would expect me to have done a little research. Then again, if I told him I had accessed the architect's computer records in order to study the layout, I could expect to find myself frog-marched out of the building.

5

"I'LL BE FRANK WITH YOU—AND DON'T TAKE THIS PERSONALLY—THE job we're offering is not vital to our operation."

I am facing Willard Thorn across the desk in his office. He has my résumé in front of him. Not that he has paid much attention to it. The glass partition beside us looks out into the control hub, but the blinds are folded too steeply for me to see anything but the floor. Even when I followed him along the gallery's closed balcony to reach his office, I didn't dare show too much interest in what is housed inside.

"The agency told me you're looking for someone presentable who is prepared to work nights."

"That just about sums it up." Willard Thorn seems almost embarrassed. "The system technology can take care of itself, but the clients like to know that there's a human face behind it at all times. If they thought the place was abandoned after dark, we'd risk losing their confidence. The same guy's held the post since we opened five years ago, but Wilson has opted to move on, and who can blame him? Let's face it, there's more to life than toggling through monitors all night long. It's especially tough when you know the system has that task covered as well. Then again, this isn't the only job where a computer calls the shots. Most of the planes that come and go from the airport are controlled by automatic pilot, but then you wouldn't get a passenger on the plane if the cockpit was empty." Thorn holds my gaze as he speaks, as if searching for some hint of disillusion.

"The job description called it a security position."

"Technically it is," he replies somewhat uncomfortably, "but the building takes care of all that, both defensively and offensively."

"Offensively?" I want to check that I heard him correctly. For this is not something I had uncovered in my preparation for the interview. "You don't hear that every day about four walls and a roof."

Thorn appears to consider what he has just told me.

"Sphinx Cargo boasts a high level of intelligence in its architecture," he says eventually. "The computer is hardwired into the structure, with the capacity to act and react at will. Think of it as a central nervous system. Everything from the CCTV cameras to the ambient environment is monitored electronically. Even the goddamn plumbing is plugged into the grid. If a fire breaks out, the computer will evaluate whether it can be extinguished by sprinklers alone. If not, she'll isolate the area and pump it with nitrogen. The gas is nonflammable, so as well as squeezing out the oxygen it also starves the flames. At any one time she knows exactly what is going on inside and out. If the software for the crane network requires an update, she'll carry it out without request. Should a client arrive without an appointment, she'll use visual recognition to be sure the correct cargo is prepared for inspection or dispatch before they've even stepped through the door."

"That's amazing," I say. "I had no idea."

"Quite literally, this building would've seen you coming. Sara might be the one to buzz you in, but not before the building has cleared you. She really is primed for every eventuality. With pressure mats under every pallet, shelf, and box, nothing can be picked up without authorization." He stops there for a moment, pausing for thought. "Let's just say if anyone was tempted to help themselves to something small like a gemstone, she'd immediately make them subject to aggressive countermeasures."

As he speaks, I am struck by how he repeatedly refers to the building as female.

"What's that old saying?" I ask after a moment. "Hell hath no fury like a woman scorned."

"I like that." Thorn grins, much to my relief, and then refers to my résumé once more. As he studies it, his expression sobers once more. "So currently you're a night guard at the Natural History Museum. Why are you thinking of moving on?"

"Sphinx Cargo is closer to home," I say. "Also, if I may be frank with you, my girlfriend works the graveyard shift at the airport. It means we'll be able to travel to and from work together. As a night watch, I like to make sure she's safe and sound."

Setting my résumé to one side, Willard Thorn sits back in his chair.

"I like your honesty, Finn. I really do. The last two guys told me just what I wanted to hear. Yes, I need someone trustworthy and with impeccable references. Someone who isn't going to sleep on the job, drink, or do drugs, and I should tell you now," he adds, leveling with me, it seems, "every restroom in the building will automatically test your urine each time you pay a visit."

I show him my palms. "I have no problem with any of this."

"The fact is, this building won't allow anyone to veer from the rules. You may lack the physical beef of the other candidates, but Sphinx can handle herself just fine in that respect. And as you're doing this in the name of love, that tells me a great deal." He rises to his feet, outstretching his hand. "Wilson is due to sign out a week from now. I'd need you to start real soon so he can bring you up to speed."

Grinning, I stand and shake his hand. "I've been with the agency for quite some time. They can pull strings to have me come across whenever it suits you."

The security director escorts me to the door. "Be here just before six tomorrow evening. After that, the computer seals the building from the outside world. We can get out, but nobody gets in. Not even the president of the goddamn company."

EVERYONE KNOWS ME BY MY ASSUMED NAME. IT'S SECOND NATURE now. After a year of this life, it's fully programmed into my system.

Only one person calls me Carl. I know this is not the smartest of moves. Uttered in the wrong place, it could earn me a place in hell. Having spent some time in a military detainment camp, I know what horrors I would face should I be recaptured and returned. Even so, hearing my real name every now and then helps to remind me who I am.

And the same thing goes for Beth.

"You woke me," she says, on opening the front door. Wrapped in a terry-cloth robe, my fellow escapee and current flatmate steps aside to let me in. "Do I smell bullion?"

"He got the job," I say, purposely ignoring her question.

"Who?"

"Who do you think?" I shake off my jacket, still damp from

the earlier downpour. "Finn Carter is now an employee of Sphinx Cargo."

Beth seems to wake up at the news. "So we're in business?"

"You know I'm not there for the gold," I say. "I'm there because it's the last place they'd think to look for me. You've seen the psychological profile they've drawn up. The conclusion is that having broken into one bullion vault I wouldn't risk a second bite of the cherry. They claim I'm a cautious operator—and they're right. Why would someone with my build get a job inside a place like Sphinx? It's too reckless for words! Which makes it about the safest place on earth, as far as I'm concerned. It's the eye of the storm."

"You said the same thing about coming to England." Beth tightens the sash around her gown and heads for the kitchenette. I grimace at what I've just told her, for I know she's not comfortable being here. As a Brit, it made sense that I should hide out on home territory. Before attempting to hack into any computer system, I'd have to learn precisely how it works—it's the only way to minimize the risk of detection—and the same approach applied here. I've spent eighteen years on this soil. I know how to go to ground so we will not be found.

Following this line of thinking, of course, Beth should've been living her new life back in Tennessee.

I hear the sound of the kettle heating up and join her in the kitchenette. She's fixing a coffee with her back to me. First thing, Beth is never good without a caffeine hit. It might be sundown outside, but for us it's time to go to work. The world is a quieter place after dark—and that suits both of us just fine.

"I know it's not ideal," I say, "but you have to trust me. I'm working toward something that's more precious to us than all the gold on offer inside Sphinx. All I'm asking for is time."

She doesn't respond for a moment, just pours the water instead. I feel awkward, standing so close behind her in this atmosphere. The kitchenette is really only big enough for one of us in here. The front room isn't much larger. We're on the seventh floor, within earshot of the highway and just three bus stops to the airport. Our apartment, like the building itself, is rough around the edges but the one place on this earth where we can breathe freely. By choice, we have no phone line or Internet connection. Not even a cell phone between us. In this electronic age, it makes us invisible to the world around.

"Time is what troubles me," Beth says eventually, and turns, nursing a steaming mug. "In my job, I see armed police and antiterror personnel wherever I look. I'm just not sure how much more I can take. My constant fear is that one of them is going to take a second glance at the young lady restocking shelves and recognize my face."

"No way," I say. "You have the correct papers and a watertight backstory. The evidence is online for anyone who cares to look."

I give her a moment to remind herself of the efforts I made to back up our new identities. Beth might have used her underworld contacts to acquire our passports, but it was me who sat in the cybercafés and breathed life into them. Through careful manipulation of everything from birth registers to school records, local news feature archives and employment databases, I created virtual paper trails for two entirely fictitious people. I even went so far as to plant evidence to suggest I had undergone plastic surgery to change my appearance radically. If attention turned to either of us, we have perfectly rehearsed lives that offer nothing of suspicion. I know Beth understands this. Looking at her now, however, I can see she's increasingly unhappy with it.

"The people we're pretending to be might appear convincing," she says next, "but we both know Beth wouldn't settle for this."

"Beth is dead," I cut in harshly. "We faked the whole thing to take away the kind of heat you're worrying about."

She sighs to herself, clearly unconvinced. "For all the stunts you pull online, Carl, every bogus e-mail, switched photograph, and fabricated dossier, the whole thing could fall apart if the people involved held a simple conversation."

"But that's just it," I remind her. "In this day and age, large organizations rely on technology to communicate through the ranks. It's a case of Telephone. At some point, if the message becomes distorted, it just carries on being copied from one department to the next. All I'm doing is adding a distortion to the message. Sure, if the generals actually sat down with the search teams who discovered the corpse, they'd discover it wasn't you. I just felt certain that would never happen. It meant we could bury some poor casualty of the uprising in the snow, knowing that the coroner's report was all that mattered. It made no odds that the team found the body of a male mercenary. As soon as I intercepted the report and made the necessary changes, you were as good as gone."

"Gone but not forgotten," she says. "Somehow I think we'll be looking over our shoulders for the rest of our days."

"I'm working on that," I remind her. "Now that I'm inside Sphinx, things are going to change for us. All you have to do is relax. Face it, Beth, America's Most Wanted tend to be living, breathing badasses like me."

Beth smiles a little despite herself. I make a face at her, and she grins outright.

"Then let's hope you can live up to your promises." She chuckles. "Else I might just grow tired of waiting and finish you for real."

7

MANTIS TATTOO STUDIO, HARAJUKU DISTRICT, TOKYO, JAPAN

THE TATTOO ARTIST WORKS BY HAND; CROSS-LEGGED AND WITHOUT a word. His client, middle-aged but pale and doughy like a seal pup, lies facedown on a mat before him. His head is turned away, with a towel folded lengthwise under his neck for support. The artist, a master in the art of tebori tattooing, finds two ribs. He spreads the skin with his thumb and forefinger, and then positions the chisel-like instrument at a shallow angle between them. The handle is fashioned from bamboo, while the tip is a hollow needle, sterilized by a lighter flame and then dipped in ink. With a jabbing motion, the artist punctures the skin. It's a process he repeats several times to drive in the color pigment. Blood and ink pool together, which he wipes once with a paper towel, before repeating the process.

The man he's working on is naked but for a loincloth.

The base of his spine is glistening with sweat.

His eyelids are heavy, zoned from the pain as the ink-dipped needle repeatedly punctures his skin. Above the pair, a ceiling fan cuts through the humid air. Judging by the designs adorning his body—the centerpiece illustrating a samurai battling a tiger among bamboo and cherry blossoms—the man has clearly endured many, many hours of suffering for his art.

As the tattooist works on this final section of space, it's clear that he doesn't have much further to go.

This work-in-progress has been artfully placed with the contours of the client's body. Both man and beast twist and rise from the foliage beginning at the back of his thighs and wrap around his waist and upper torso. Despite the scale of the piece, everything cuts off abruptly at the neck, the wrists, and the ankles. For this is a traditional yakuza body suit. On completion, it will mark him out as a general among Japan's infamous criminal network.

It is raining heavily outside. Guttering water, voices, and car horns fill the air. In the market below this second-story studio, people are resigned to the downpour. Notably, one such figure can be seen cutting across the ebb and flow. He's broadly built, clearly Western, and sports a grizzled gray beard. Wearing a baggy, shapeless anorak he should look quite world-weary. As it is, this frowning figure walks with such purpose that people make way for him. He pauses only to glance up at the second-story window, and then takes to the stairs.

The tattooist is completing the color fill. He's shading in a waterfall. It plunges over rocks, in the background to the great fight, and pools just above his subject's pelvic bone.

When the man with the beard appears in the studio, slipping off his shoes at the top, the tattooist silently acknowledges his presence. He does not stop his work, however. Not until this looming figure has padded around him and then collected each end of the towel beneath his client's neck.

Moving swiftly but surely, the Westerner crosses his hands and pulls tight. With a gasp of surprise and a gurgle, the client on the mat reaches for the band now crushing his windpipe. His attacker is one step ahead, however. He drives one foot into the small of the client's back, pinning him there and pulling yet tighter on the towel.

At first the Westerner shows no sign of the effort he is making to strangle the man. Slowly but surely, however, as his victim's flailing attempts to free himself grow weaker, he begins to grit his teeth and grimace. Even when the man falls limp, he continues to hold the towel in position for a full minute.

"*Sayonara*, sunshine," he whispers finally, in a gravel-scarred voice that reveals his North American origin.

All this time the tattooist watches him intently. There is no doubt that he has been expecting this visit. He shows no emotion when the killer releases his lifeless victim and slips the towel from his neck. When their eyes finally meet, the tattooist gestures at the corpse with his tapping stick. He lifts his eyebrows hopefully.

Massaging his palms, the bearded figure offers his consent with a slight bow. He steps away from his victim, appraising his own handiwork, before heading down the stairs back out into the downpour.

For a moment the tattoo artist sits in contemplation. Then, with a sigh, he resumes his work, tapping in the last detail of this body suit as a final mark of respect.

8

A WEEK AFTER I "KILLED" BETH AND WE WENT TO GROUND TOGETHER
on the European mainland, I realized that I couldn't stop
thinking about her. As she watched me at work in backstreet
cybercafés, securing our safe passage home, I discovered that she
felt the same way too. She might have successfully conned me
into opening the doors at Fort Knox so she could plunder the
vault, but the trouble it had landed us in bound us together.

Things aren't easy between us, of course. After just three
weeks on the run, while I continued to work on our virtual identities so that we could travel freely, Beth left a note and disappeared. On her return, several days later, I was deeply unsettled
by the stack of euros she pressed into my hand. Her business was
not mine, she had insisted so sharply. I figured the sum was hot
as hell. But despite having my heart in my mouth as I converted
it into home currency, her money brought us to where we are
now. The flat is cramped and depressing, but we both know that

nothing compares to the hell of the cages we'd been kept in at the detainment camp. What's more, despite the tension, together it feels like there must be a brighter future awaiting us.

On passing through the security pod at Sphinx Cargo, ready for my first night shift, I feel as if I'm a step closer to finding out.

"Right on time." Between the feet of the majestic statue, Sara Sinclair is already climbing into her coat. As she does so, she taps at the keyboard and glances at her monitor. "We're delighted that you're joining us, Finn."

I smile brightly, despite the fact that she's evidently had to remind herself of my name. "It's great to be here," I say, arriving at the reception desk. "It makes a change from spending the night among stuffed animals and dinosaur bones."

She looks at me quizzically, buttoning herself up, and then refers to the monitor once more. "Oh, I see. Your former position." This time, she makes no effort to hide the fact that my details are onscreen. "Hey, you're an Aries. Same as my boyfriend."

I grin at her, signing in as I do so. "What else do you know about me?"

Sara Sinclair considers me with some amusement and then sinks into her seat. She moves her mouse into what I take to be a password field. I watch her fingertips peck at the keyboard, quietly pleased to see the sequence I had anticipated. After a moment, having clicked through several folders, she arches one eyebrow. "Without wishing to be rude, you should ask for a pay raise."

"I haven't done any work yet!" I laugh. "But maybe you can put a good word in once I've completed my trial period."

"I'll do just that." Logging out of her computer once more, Sara Sinclair gathers her bag from under the desk. At the same time, the sound of a door popping open draws our attention to the top of the stairs. From the airlock steps an older man whose tie and blazer immediately tells me this must be my colleague for the night.

"Hey, Sara, honey, I have a tip for your other half."

I glance across at her. She rolls her eyes and mutters, "The horses."

"Maitresse is riding tomorrow at Haydock. The odds are high, but if the going is heavy she should romp home."

Sara Sinclair nods, but it's clear to me that she isn't listening. "Wilson, this is Finn," she calls back, her voice echoing in the majestic expanse. "He lists his interests as running. That's the only sport he entered. I didn't see anything about horse racing, so go easy on him, eh?"

The man called Wilson chuckles to himself and invites me to join him upstairs. "I'll see you tomorrow morning," I say, turning back to Sara.

"He likes to talk," she says under her breath.

"That's fine," I reply, thinking at the same time that this is going much better than I could have planned. "I'm a good listener."

In the background, the sound of an incoming aircraft begins to build. I turn to climb the staircase. As the plane roars overhead, I pay it no attention whatsoever.

For I have a job to do, and nothing can distract me now.

9

I PLACE WILSON SOMEWHERE IN HIS EARLY FIFTIES. HIS NEAT, PRESSED uniform does little to soften a notably weather-beaten face. One shaped by the elements, alcohol, or both, I think. Still, he welcomes me warmly, keeping my gaze as he shakes my hand. Sizing up his replacement, it seems.

"So you're a runner," he says, as we leave the airlock for the walkway. He moves briskly, but with some stiffness in one leg. "What kind of running?"

In the back of my mind, I think about telling him I've been running from the CIA and the American military for the last twelve months. Instead, I say, "Mostly the streets and the parks."

"You're not a gym bunny, then?"

"Treadmills aren't my thing," I say. "I like to feel fresh air in my lungs."

He glances over his shoulder, grinning. "You won't find much of that in here."

Wilson leads me into the gallery, through the airlock at the far end. In front of us, a spiral staircase winds down through the central support column. On my last visit, Willard Thorn had turned right along the balcony corridor and then through a door into the control hub itself. This time, Wilson takes me left along the corridor. Overlooking the main storage area, we pass alongside a closed office area with lights on low and half a dozen desks. Each one has a flat screen, keyboard, and telephone.

"Client services," says Wilson. "The building can handle the import and export side of things just fine, but people like to speak to people when it comes to doing business. I certainly wouldn't want to check in millions of pounds' worth of freight using an automated system, no matter how good it is."

"So the personnel in this section are here for the sake of appearance, just like us?"

Wilson reaches a door at the far end. Grasping the handle, he turns to face me. "Pretty much. Only those guys at least interact with the clients. Where we're heading is bottom of the food chain."

The door opens up onto another spiral staircase. Winding our way down, I find three rooms arranged around the foot of this column. Wilson opens each door in turn. One is dark, but illuminated by a wall of CCTV monitors. Another is fitted with a microwave, sink, and fridge. The final door opens onto a locker space and a toilet cubicle.

"I thought my flat was cramped," I say, peering around at my surroundings.

"Welcome to my world," he says. "You'll find your uniform inside the locker. I'll give you a minute to sort yourself out."

Wilson closes the door behind me. A glance around confirms one thing about Wilson's domain. Unlike the sophisticated security to be found throughout the rest of the building, only one camera covers the whole area. It's mounted on the ceiling at the foot of the stairs. As Wilson showed me around, I noted it rotating slowly but steadily through three hundred and sixty degrees.

As I change, I dwell on the fact that in every secure system there is an Achilles' heel. Almost every time, that weak point is human. In this case, someone had made the decision to install just one camera down here. As the individual in charge of monitoring the building would only be watching himself, perhaps it just wasn't deemed necessary. Evidently there is nothing worth stealing from these three tucked-away rooms, but the blind spots it created would be invaluable to me.

I find Wilson in the monitoring room. He's at his chair, peaked hat on the desk, sipping at a mug of tea. I take the seat behind him and thank him for the brew he's made for me.

"Five years is some achievement," I say. "What's kept you in the job for so long?"

Wilson smiles to himself and then turns to a filing cabinet

behind him. From the top drawer, he pulls out a thick manuscript bound with elastic bands. "I like to write," he says. "Write and reflect."

He places the paper stack on his lap. I glance at the title, but he covers it almost bashfully with one hand.

"Is it autobiographical?" I ask.

Wilson nods. "I joined the army straight out of school. The Falklands was my first tour of duty." He pauses there for a moment and pats his bad leg. "Also my last."

In the silence that follows, I wish I hadn't raised the question in the first place.

"Are you hoping to have it published?" I ask, trying to move along the conversation.

With a fond pat, Wilson returns the manuscript to the drawer. "When it's done," he tells me, sounding wistful now. "First I need to find me some new employment."

I catch my breath when he says this, and do nothing to hide my surprise. "I was told you were moving on. I assumed you had something lined up!"

Wilson smiles at this. "That would've been nice. If only they'd given me the time to look."

"They're kicking you out?"

Returning to his mug of tea, Wilson addresses me while looking at the monitors.

"Not *them*, exactly," he says. "The building."

I wait for him to face me.

"This *place* has suggested that you leave?"

Wilson rasps his chin with one hand. "I've made some errors lately. We all know computers don't like errors. In the case of this particular error, it's something that a younger man like you is less likely to repeat."

"What did you do?" I ask.

"I fell asleep. Right here in this seat. Not once, but three times in a month."

"Is that all? You took a nap?"

"On each occasion the motion sensors picked it up, and that's when alarm bells ring. The building provides a regular threat analysis for Willard and the bosses back in the States. I guess I must have tested her patience, because my name cropped up as a weak point in the system. Willard has been good to me over the years, but this left him no choice."

"I'm really sorry," I say after a moment. "And there's nothing you can do to change their mind?"

Wilson waves away the suggestion, finishing his tea. "When Cleopatra speaks, her word is final."

I have just swigged from my own mug when he says this, and almost choke in the process. *"Who?"*

10

DAMNOEN SADUAK FLOATING MARKET, BANGKOK, THAILAND

WITH HIS COFFEE SERVED, THE WESTERNER APPRECIATES THE VIEW from a terrace overlooking the canal. Below, the waterway is crammed with small boats. Most are laden with fruit and vegetables, paddled by traders in bamboo hats. Others pilot both locals and tourists. Exchanges take place on the water and with the bustling crowd on the banks. The atmosphere is one of organized chaos.

Today he's wearing a rumpled linen suit jacket with a pair of sunglasses slotted inside the top pocket. He closes his eyes for a moment, the sun beating on his brow and beard. When he opens them, he notes the approach of a gangly, awkward-looking man clutching a satchel. The guy weaves around the tables, pushing his spectacles back in place and apologizing to those who have to draw in their chairs so he can pass.

"One time," he mutters, on falling into the seat beside the man in the jacket, "it would be good to meet someplace where I speak the language."

The bearded individual he has just joined, a bounty hunter by the name of Samuel Ramsay, appears to be in no hurry to answer. He sips his coffee, his attention on the waterway.

"Are you wearing a wire?" he asks finally.

The man with the satchel looks at him incredulously. "Why do you ask?"

"You're CIA," he says. "As an ex-employee, I wouldn't leave my hotel room without one."

The man mops his neck with a handkerchief, and then signals for a coffee. "I'm not wearing a wire, Samuel. My career might put me in an early grave, but I do value my life."

Samuel Ramsay smiles at the remark. "Relax," he says. "Even if you *were* lying to me, I wouldn't kill you. That would leave just the bad guys to hire me. I'm not sure that would sit so well on my conscience."

The man from the CIA opens up his satchel. "Carl Hobbes," he says matter-of-factly, and draws out a folder. "Heard the name? Al-Qaeda won't forget him in a hurry."

Ramsay sips his coffee. "How much is he worth?"

"Twenty million."

The man from the CIA hands him the folder, quietly pleased

that he has the full attention of this murkiest of his contacts. Back in the day, when they worked in the same department, Ramsay cut a clean appearance. As well as the beard, he's put a little weight on over the years, and in many ways he wears it well. He doesn't look like the covert and calculating bounty hunter for hire that he has become. In the same way, it came as a complete shock to the organization when evidence surfaced that Ramsay was selling information to the very terror cells he was supposed to hunt down. On record, he had simply vanished when his treachery was discovered. In reality, the CIA knew how to find him if ever his services were required.

"That's an impressive sum," observes Ramsay now, leafing through the papers inside, "for a computer hacker."

"Hobbes also played a central role in the Camp Twilight breakout—"

"Messy business." Ramsay tuts to himself, interrupting the man. "Some good guys were lost there. On both sides."

"And the fact that he's running free is a scandal in the making. If the American people find out he's at liberty to cripple the country at a keystroke, there would be hell to pay."

"Excuse me for speaking my mind," adds Ramsay, examining a mug shot now, "but the kid hardly fits that description."

"Maybe not in the real world. Online, as far as the administration is concerned, he's the Great Satan. Hobbes has evaded capture for so long now that their patience with us has run out. Personally, I did hold the view that he's already dead, though the powers that be think otherwise. They're throwing money at the problem, which is madness in my view, knowing the people it'll attract."

"Don't be so down on the bounty hunters." Ramsay continues to flick through the folder. "Maybe some of us play a little rough, but we're all just earning a living, same as you."

"All I want is Hobbes in our custody and removed from my list of problems. This is why I've come to you first, Samuel. I really don't care how you bring him in, but if you're going to take the job I suggest you move fast. Al-Qaeda is all out for vengeance. They hold the boy personally responsible for the loss of a mercenary hired by them at great expense."

"Christian McCoy." Ramsay scratches at his beard. "Their loss has been my gain. Since his demise I've picked up several commissions that would've gone to him."

The man from the CIA shows him his palms. "I don't want to know. Samuel, give me a break. I'm out here unofficially as it is." He draws breath to continue, only to wait as his coffee is served. When he does speak, he leans in and keeps his voice low. "During Saddam Hussein's final years in power, you may recall how he created a hit squad of female assassins. These lethal ladies were dispatched across Europe as actresses and dancers seeking asylum. In reality, their mission was to target Iraqi dissidents who had fled the country—"

"—seduce them into revealing their activities, and then kill them."

Ramsay finishes the assessment while looking out across the canal. He looks bored, as if perhaps he is wise to this story from his time at the CIA.

"After Saddam's reign ended," continues the man briefing him, having cleared his throat, "the hit squad fragmented and basically melted away. According to our intelligence, Al-Qaeda's latest daughter of death is none other than Saddam's personal favorite throughout those brutal years."

Samuel Ramsay faces around to him. "Sabine? Sabine-i-Sabah is still operating?"

"None other."

Ramsay chuckles and shakes his head. "Then Hobbes is as good as dead."

"Not if you act now, Samuel."

"At least with me I guess you have a choice whether the kid survives."

"That's precisely why I've come to you," replies the man from the CIA. "Your loyalty to whoever waves the dollars in your face is indisputable. I know for the bounty on offer you'd have no problem killing Hobbes, but the deal is we want him in one piece. When it comes to hacking, the boy is bleeding edge. We need him to show us just how he's been manipulating our systems, which is why it's vital that you get to him before the Al-Qaeda assassin."

"So," says Ramsay, closing the folder, "where will I find Master Hobbes? Just looking through the paperwork here tells me he could be anywhere on the planet."

"We're ninety percent sure the majority of sightings have been fabricated by him online. So far he's outwitted us all. I trust he won't make the same fool out of you."

"When was his last known sighting?"

"Hobbes escaped from Camp Twilight with an accomplice, Beth Nelson. She didn't take kindly to the extreme cold. Breathed her last just beyond the perimeter. Hobbes laid her to rest in the snow. It would be touching, but since then he's been a ghost to us."

The bounty hunter dwells on this, watching the boats go by.

"I knew Beth," he says. "She had ambition. Lot of bullion bars for sale as well." The man from the CIA does not respond. "The girl sure carried ice in her heart, but I'm surprised she let the cold claim it entirely. If anyone had been destined for greater things, it was her."

"Well, she's going nowhere now." He gestures at the file. "You'll find some shots from the scene in the autopsy report.

Hypothermia is no way to die. I'd rather burn than freeze off my behind."

Samuel Ramsay searches through the documentation. He draws out what he's looking for and considers the image for a moment. Then he smiles to himself, shaking his head at the same time.

"She's alive," he states, and flops the photograph onto the table. "Look at her lashes, man. Where's the frost?" The man from the CIA looks at the image, adjusting his glasses unnecessarily. "The makeup is as convincing as the report, but they've both been fabricated for your benefit, and I think I know how you guys fell for it. This is a fake, my friend. She's playing dead, most probably well after the event, but the hacker kid knew you wouldn't ask questions because it came in through official channels." Leaving him silenced, the bounty hunter folds several dollar bills for the waiter under his coffee cup and rises from his chair. "If you want me to get to Hobbes before Sabine, this is all I need to know."

11

THE MOMENT WILSON CLICKS OPEN THE DOOR INTO THE CONTROL hub, several ceiling-mounted cameras swivel round to point at us.

"Don't be alarmed," says Wilson. "We're authorized to come in here. Cleopatra will have amassed all the visual recognition markers she needs to verify who you are. Just don't touch anything."

I stand beside him, struck by the spectacle at the center of this dimly lit room. Normally, I'd expect to find up to half a dozen towering servers humming away. Here, I'm looking up at a looming pyramid, at least twice my height, constructed from brushed aluminium and tempered, sloping glass walls. Inside, the multiprocessor components hum and blink.

"I've never seen anything like it," I say, and I really mean it. For I know from my research that what I'm looking at here is a *super*computer. A specialist system dedicated to tackling one specific objective. Constructed to crunch huge amounts of information, these tailor-made leviathans often possess the power to find their own solutions to whatever task they have been programmed to undertake. Instruct a supercomputer in the basic rules of chess and within a short space of time it would be ready to face down a grandmaster. Provide all the telescopic images of deep space ever taken and it will begin to map the universe.

In this case, the sole aim of this spectacular pyramid is to maintain the security of the building in which it is housed.

"Cleo is one of a kind," says Wilson, breaking the silence now. "She's an impressive piece of work, even if she has no use for me any longer." As he speaks, I turn my attention to the control desk in front of the pyramid. Glass-topped, with two flat-screen monitors and a high-backed leather chair, the desk is designed for a single operator. One screen displays several columns of fast-changing digits. The other shows a top-down digital wireframe of the entire building. I come closer for a better look. Inside the rectangle denoting the room we're in, two green lights are blinking.

"If the light turns red," jokes Wilson, "be afraid."

"Has that ever happened?"

"It might next week," he says, "if I show up for work."

I smile in sympathy and then ask if it's okay to look over the pyramid. Wilson seems to weigh this in his mind for a moment. "I think perhaps not just yet," he says. "Cleo will be tracking your moves as we speak, recording our conversations and building up a behavioral profile. It's fine for me to show you around, but I really wouldn't show too much interest in anything of value."

I stand back, taking in the structure. "You mean I have to *earn her confidence?*"

"I suppose you do." Wilson retreats to the door now. "Why don't we give her a chance to assess you?" he says. "She requires me to make one physical inspection of the premises each shift. We can do it now, if you like."

"Cleopatra has no reason to be wary." I glance back as one of the overhead cameras whirs around to follow me out onto the gallery corridor. "I really am one of the good guys."

During the course of my research, mostly carried out in the quietest corner of my local library, I discovered as much as I could about Sphinx Cargo. When I wasn't throwing my pursuers off the scent, popping up on virtual radars from Atlanta to Zanzibar, I sought to understand a security system that had intrigued me from the moment I learned of its existence. I had Beth to thank for this. With a coffee stand located beside the perfume store, she often picked up on interesting conversations between business passengers in transit. Naturally, for someone of her nature, the mention of bullion bars caused her ears to perk up. What prompted me to make further investigations was the talk she overheard about the technology that had gone into guarding it.

Online, I absorbed everything about Sphinx Cargo that was on public record. Having visited a stylishly minimal website, I called client services to test how they handled a potential storage inquiry. Then I worked on accessing information that should have been out of bounds. I cracked the database containing the architect's original plans, while a slightly sleepy session reading up on Sphinx Cargo's insurance contract unearthed gold in the form of a risk assessor's report. What was supposed to be an evaluation of the company's ability to cope with setbacks such as fire, flood, or theft instead confirmed to me that this really was one of the most intelligent computer systems I had ever encountered. It meant I wasn't just familiar with the building's interior before I'd even stepped inside. I also knew that the computer at its heart called every single shot.

Despite the high-end technology, the recruitment process was a human affair. On discovering that Sphinx Cargo sourced its low-level personnel from the same agency, I seized the opportunity for my way in. First, I enrolled in a course to qualify for my security guard license. The course was only a weekend long, and along with genuine accreditation, I figured the insight into the profession would be useful. Next, with a carefully constructed résumé, complete with e-mail addresses for references that would all be routed back to me, I applied for work at the agency. During the interview, I expressed an interest in Sphinx. When my interviewer registered my details, for nothing was available at the time, I carefully arranged myself so I could read the company's contact name on the account screen.

It was in between shifts at the Natural History Museum, a post I accepted through the agency, that I befriended Sara Sinclair.

A brief online search of her name told me Sara was an enthusiastic user of social network sites. Within a week of fabricating a personal profile and extending an invite to Sara that she could not resist, I had coaxed enough information to be confident that she used the same password for every secure site she visited. Not just at home, as I had gone on to confirm, but also in the workplace.

At some point in the future, once I'd fulfilled the challenge set for myself, I intended to warn her not to be so quick to accept strangers as her friends. During the course of our correspondence, a month or so later, I learned that a position at her workplace was imminent. That's when I prepared myself to make the best impression by slipping onto the recruitment agency database and assessing the competition.

As a hacker, I couldn't have secured the job without such extensive preparation. It had taken months of my time. Even so, as I follow Wilson along the balcony corridor, I know that I have really only scratched the surface. Nowhere had I learned that the supercomputer inside the building possessed a name, or that its capabilities extended to taking offensive measures against any assault. Although I had already breached the system's front end, by tapping into Willard Thorn's faith in human involvement, the lack of available intelligence on Cleopatra told me she was really something very special indeed.

On leaving the control hub behind, I feel sure that she and I would work wonders together. It was just a question of finding the opportunity to become acquainted.

"Has she ever made an error?" I ask, following Wilson as he makes his way toward the central stairwell.

He pauses at the rail to think about this. A wry smile crosses his lips.

"In my view, she screwed up by reporting me as a security risk," he says. "But I can see she's already found a worthy replacement."

12

FROM THE ARCHITECT'S PLANS, I ALREADY KNOW THE WINDING STAIRS right in front of us will take us to the floor of the main storage area. I am also aware that the third column houses the backup generator. In the event of a power blackout, Sphinx could produce her own juice from the solar panels to keep everything running indefinitely. I am keen to visit every area. I want to work out how it all comes together to function as a system. At this moment, however, as my guide reaches the foot of the stairs, I make every effort to look as if everything is quite new to me.

"Another airlock," I say, as Wilson opens a locker beside it.

"Take this." He hands me a tank the size of a small fire extinguisher, with a shoulder holster and a transparent mask. "I suggest you put it on now, unless you want to pass out on your first night in the job."

Together we snap on our breathing apparatus. When Wilson asks if I am ready, his voice sounds like it's coming from behind a closed door. I hear him clearly enough, however, and accept the flashlight that he hands me.

As soon as the airlock opens, I realize just how vast this space really is. In the gloom, such precisely spaced pallet stacks appear to stretch away endlessly. We step out onto the floor, firing up our flashlights one after the other.

"It can feel like a labyrinth at first," Wilson tells me. "But you'll soon learn to find your way around."

Overhead, the walkway reaches across from one airlock to the other. The studded floor lights make it look like some kind of docking tunnel between two spacecraft. I switch the beam between towering stacks, in awe of what I see on each shelf.

"Some of this stuff looks priceless," I say.

"Another reason not to get too close." Wilson invites me to follow him between the central stacks. "Even if you tried, Cleopatra could choose to stop you dead."

"How so?"

"By reasonable force," he tells me matter-of-factly. "You name it, she's got it covered." As he speaks, a robotic arm glides gracefully across the pallet intersection in front of us. I hoist my flashlight high and see the circular gears at work in the ceiling. "She also likes to have everything stored neatly at the end of each working day."

I realize that several other arms are also steering through the passageways and turn to see one pass through the intersection behind me. Then, in perfect synchronicity, they all stop in their tracks and retract into the darkness.

"Is she in sleep mode now?"

Wilson shakes his head and continues moving through the passage. "Cleopatra *never* sleeps. Perhaps that's why she has such a problem with me."

I follow Wilson without a word. At every intersection he sweeps his flashlight left and right, and so I do the same thing. On reaching the end, he appears to lead me on a random path back through the pallets. I follow quietly, just taking in the sight of so many treasures.

Then Wilson halts abruptly at an intersection and snaps his flashlight crossways.

"What's up?" I draw up beside him, feeling suddenly quite alarmed.

Wilson doesn't answer for a moment. "Thought I heard something," he says, speaking low through his face mask. "It could be that they're back."

I face him side on but receive no explanation. Without a word, Wilson creeps along the passageway. He motions for me to follow. I watch him advance for a moment and then hurry to keep up. As we draw toward the side of the building, he raises his hand for me to halt. He's trained his flashlight on the floor several pallets ahead.

I am about to press for an explanation when the rat scuttles into view.

It seems unaware of our presence, halting just outside the circle of light. Then another one emerges, crossing between pallets now.

"Is there a problem with vermin in here?" I ask in a whisper.

"Not for long," Wilson replies under his breath. "Watch."

I focus on the two rats. One is cleaning its whiskers. The other has sensed our presence, I think, because it rises up onto its haunches to sniff the air.

A moment later both animals are twitching on their sides, and I am lost for words.

A coil of smoke hangs over each of them, dispersing as they fall still. It's the only evidence of the blue bolts of electricity that have just struck them. I face Wilson, and then look back at the lifeless creatures as if to check that I'm not mistaken.

"Cleo is an efficient pest controller, wouldn't you agree?"

"Where did *that* come from?" I ask, my heart still hammering from the shock. Each bolt had originated from high behind us, spitting down over our heads. I turn and look around. Wilson watches me with some amusement.

"The underside of the walkway is fitted with discrete electroshock cannons," he says, and sweeps the structure with his flashlight. "Basically, those rats each got hit by a minuscule needle carrying a massive electric charge. We're talking about something no bigger than a wasp sting that can pack a rhinoceros punch."

"I had no idea such a device existed," I say, peering up at the walkway.

"It's a prototype countermeasure, but the company just cannot afford to let vermin sink their teeth into anything here. Cleo is in charge of keeping the problem under control. Her motion detectors pick up on their presence straightaway. After that, if they're in the open they fry, and should they take refuge under the pallets she flushes them out by playing a high-pitched frequency through the speaker system."

"Where do they get in?"

"Loading chamber." Bringing his flashlight back down, Wilson shines it over the dead rats. Just above ground level, I see a huge steel shutter span the far end of the passage. With my own flashlight, I realize that this is a section of a vast hatch. "When the exterior shutter is open they sometimes climb into the airlock," he explains. "In some ways it's a blessing Cleo deals with them so swiftly. They'd only face a slow death from lack of oxygen otherwise."

I look back up at the walkway. "Would she use the cannons on people?"

"She can regulate the electrical charge," he tells me. "So it's in her arsenal." Wilson steps across to the dead vermin. With a sigh, he picks them up by their tails. "One time a pigeon got in," he calls back. "Cleo had some fun with that. Mind you, there wasn't much left of it to clean up but feathers."

"You make it sound like she *enjoys* it," I say, but Wilson is out of earshot.

13

I ARRIVE AT THE AIRPORT JUST AS THE FLIGHTS BEGIN FOR THE DAY. At this hour, inside the terminal, people are clearly going places. Those who have been here overnight pick themselves up and prepare for their travels, while the check-in queues start to build and thicken. As I make my way across the concourse, all eyes are on the departure boards.

On seeing Beth, sorting paperwork at the perfume counter, I do wonder what is stopping her from simply taking off without me.

"Hey," I say, and hand her one of the coffees I've just bought for us. "Do you remember how we had that problem with the mice when we first moved in?"

"Are they back again?" Beth looks tired. She's immaculately presented, as the job requires, but I can tell from her manner that it's been another long, uneventful night.

"If they ever return," I say, "I'm going to ask Cleopatra for some tips on extreme extermination."

Beth looks at me quizzically. "Cleopatra would be who? A new colleague?"

I tell her about my first introduction to the supercomputer and how it handled the vermin. Just blew them to kingdom come before they'd had a chance to even squeak. Beth tells me to slow down and then looks over my shoulder. She waves at whoever is approaching behind me and tidies the paperwork. "My shift handover is here. Let me grab my coat and you can tell me all about it on our way back to the flat."

We sit at the back of the bus. It's drizzling outside. The windows are steamed, and the air smells of petroleum and chewing gum. The only other passengers sit near the front with their flight baggage. The seclusion leaves me free to bring Beth up to speed on what I've learned about Sphinx.

"I've never seen you sound so enthusiastic," she remarks eventually. "This place must really be something."

"Oh, it is," I agree. "The system totally exceeded my expectations."

"So when are you going to crack it and sneak me in?"

Her question isn't unexpected, but it still silences me. Looking into her eyes now, I begin to wonder if she'll ever accept my reasoning.

"Beth, I've no intention of stealing from Sphinx. If I had

designs on thieving so much as a paper clip, we might as well turn ourselves in right now. It's risk taking for all the wrong reasons."

With a sigh, Beth turns and looks out the bus window. We pass a stretch of run-down store fronts and a funeral parlor. I can't help thinking that the parlor looks livelier than the shops.

Then Beth faces me again, all fired up this time.

"The place is *crammed* with treasures—and you're one of the few people on this earth who could open it up so I can get on with what I do best." She pauses there and looks me in the eye. "I'm a bullion thief," she reminds me under her breath. "It's in my blood."

As she speaks, the bus draws up at our stop. Behind the shelter, several tower blocks loom large under a lead-gray sky. I follow her to the exit door, my mouth in a tight line, and nod at the driver on the way out. Nobody else leaves the vehicle. As it pulls away, leaving us in a veil of exhaust fumes, I steer Beth under the shelter and grasp her gently by her wrists.

"I'm not in the job to steal from Sphinx—I'm there to secure our *freedom*." I draw breath here, anxious that she recognizes the value of what this is all about. "Cleopatra is designed to protect all items inside the building by any means. I believe I can teach her to afford us the same protection on the *outside*. The way I see things, the rules are exactly the same. It's just a different playing field."

"What's wrong with simply killing yourself off? Same as you did for me."

Without giving me a chance to respond, Beth begins making her way towards our block. When I first pitched the idea, during the course of my research into the supercomputer's abilities, she reacted in the same way. All I had asked was that she give me a chance to prove that it could be done. Now I had gotten as far as earning a nocturnal post alone inside the building, and yet still I sense that she needs to be convinced.

Beth is following a path that divides a weedy, triangular green fouled by dogs. With a sigh, I hurry to catch her.

"We faked your death at a time of chaos," I say, coming up alongside her. "If I stage a similar fate for myself now, after they've been chasing me for so long, it's likely to be investigated. If they uncover the truth, and re-examine your case, we'd be right back where we started."

We approach the main doors to our block. Litter spirals in the corner, hemmed there by a downdraft.

"I just don't know how happy I am thinking that my safety could be left in the hands of a computer," she says.

"A *super*computer," I remind her, pulling open one door. "It's like having a thousand PCs working together at the same time. Even then it wouldn't compare. Cleo's programmed to make informed decisions in order to safeguard the contents of the building. Every threat, no matter how small, is analyzed and dealt with accordingly. All I need is some time to play with the software behind it so she secretly guards *us* with the same efficiency in the outside world."

"What is she? Robocop?"

"She's more effective than that," I press on. "Using just a tiny fraction of her processing power, she has the potential to monitor every trace of virtual activity relating to the hunt for us. I believe I can teach her to take steps that ensure we stay safe."

"The *potential*," she stresses, cutting across me again. "Carl, I have the potential to be president of the United States. Ain't never gonna happen, though."

"It isn't as if I'd have to start from scratch," I explain. "Cleopatra already operates by the same principles as me. I zone in on weaknesses in a secure system—and that's what she does to keep Sphinx Cargo safe and sound. The only difference between us is that I exploit those weaknesses and she strengthens them."

"So you're hoping to quietly turn her into a hacker?"

Beth shakes her head at me, as if I've just shared a crazy dream, and steps out of the drizzle.

We ride the elevator in awkward silence. It stops three floors before our level. The doors open up onto the concrete landing.

There is nobody waiting to join us. I press the button to resume the journey. The doors do not close. We wait a moment longer. Beth sighs to herself. She is also the first to get out and take the stairs. At this level, the wind gusts and buffets the building. We are used to it, howling as it does around the exterior walls of our flat. Right now, however, my surroundings feel like they are conspiring to side against me.

"I guess I'm just restless," she says as we climb the final flight. "You've set yourself up with a new challenge, Carl, but I need one just as much as you."

"Trust me," I reply. "All I ask from you is some time to prove myself. If I can pull this off, we really are free to make the most of our lives."

14

JORDAAN DISTRICT, AMSTERDAM, THE NETHERLANDS

THE COURTYARD RESTAURANT IS ACCESSED THROUGH A NARROW passage between two almshouses. Contained by whitewashed walls, ferns, and red geraniums, it is a quiet, tranquil place to escape from the bustle of the main thoroughfare.

Within this enclave, every place is set for lunch. It is not quite midday, however, and only just beginning to fill. All but one of the occupied tables are taken by couples. The lone diner is seated in the corner with a view of the passage. He studies the menu, sipping at a mineral water and scratching at the back of his neck. With his crumpled suit and mop of curly hair, the man has an air of untidiness about him. His name is Piet van den Bos. He is also known as Piet van Beverin, depending on who he's doing business with. At regular intervals, he looks up at the passage. He appears a little anxious. His table has been set for two.

When the figure with the thick graying hair and the beard appears, Piet scrapes his chair back across the cobbles in a clumsy bid to stand.

"Good to see you." Samuel Ramsay shakes the man's hand across the table. "I didn't think you would be late."

The man smiles and invites him to be seated. "With the deal you outlined," he says, "why would I miss the opportunity?"

Ramsay accepts the menu from the waiter who has appeared at his side. "Are you eating?" he asks his companion.

"Are you paying?"

With a quiet smile, Ramsay confirms that lunch is on him. "I recommend the sea bass," he tells Piet. "Simple but fresh."

Piet chooses the fish and returns the menu to the waiter. "You know Amsterdam well?" he asks.

"No better than any other city," replies Ramsay, "but I do a lot of traveling."

"I'm sure," Piet replies, and his eyes dart left and right. "Acquiring bullion is very much an international trade."

Samuel Ramsay sits back in his chair, observing the other man. His scrutiny leaves Piet looking very twitchy indeed. More so when Ramsay tells him to relax.

"That isn't easy," says Piet tetchily. "Not in my business."

"So, do you have it with you?"

Underneath the table, Piet squeezes a holdall bag between his feet.

"If you have the three hundred thousand euros. As we agreed."

"I should like to see the bar first," the bounty hunter tells him.

Piet's eyes pinch at the corners. Then he laughs out loud. It's a nervous release, which ends abruptly. "What is this," he asks, "a question of *trust*?"

For a moment, both men stare at each other. Ramsay is the first to break it. He does so with a smile. Opens his jacket and offers Piet a glimpse of the folded bills peeking from his inside pocket.

"It's all real," Ramsay assures him. "I heard what happened last time someone fed you counterfeit money."

Piet grins, revealing teeth stained by tobacco. "We have a lot of canals in this city," he says. "Sometimes people go missing." He pauses there, glances around to make sure no other diners are paying attention, and then dips down to unzip the bag.

When the man straightens up in his seat, Ramsay is sitting with his elbows on the table, both hands clasped as if preparing to say grace. "You know what?" he says. "I believe you have the genuine article down there. Anyone who deals with Beth Nelson is a friend of mine."

At once, the color in Piet's face drains. He swallows uncomfortably and reaches for the glass of mineral water. "You know Beth?"

"*Knew* Beth," Ramsay says to correct him. "May her soul rest in peace."

Spooked by this turn in the conversation, Piet gathers the handles of his bag to leave.

Gently Ramsay grasps his upper arm and tells him to be seated. "Hey," he says, "we haven't finished."

"This deal is canceled," Piet says under his breath, mindful that other diners are within earshot. "I never knew Beth."

"Level with me, Piet. When I learned the girl may have faked her death I figured I'd check out her old connections. As you're the nearest bullion launderer to where she supposedly breathed her last, it made sense to start with you. A thief of Beth's pedigree guarantees she'll have stashed away a few bars, and if she's on the run she'll need to cash them in for funds." He stops there for a moment to let the Dutchman digest this. "I'm on the money, Piet, I just know I am. The good news is that I'm not here to take the gold she sold to you. You can keep it. All I want is information. I need you to tell me where she is and who she's with."

"Forget it! I don't know what you're talking about!"

Ramsay looks entirely unfazed by the man's refusal to

cooperate. He considers Piet for a moment and then releases the grip on his arm.

"The bad news," he tells Piet, "is that the water you just drank has been poisoned. I laced it when you were busy opening up the bag for me." The bounty hunter produces a glass vial from his pocket. It contains a silvery powder. "This is thallium," he says. "It's aggressive stuff. Just a pinch can cause a cascade of damage through your nervous system—and you took quite a hit just then, Piet. One by one, over the next two weeks your organs will begin to shut down. It'll destroy your kidneys, your lungs, your pancreas, your stomach and heart."

"You're bluffing." Piet struggles to find the right words. "This didn't happen."

Ramsay plays with the vial, clearly in no hurry now.

"One time I had to bring in a pharmacist who ran a home-made bomb-making factory," he says eventually. "The guy was a nut. Had a grudge against some medicine manufacturer. I don't recall the details. Still, some of the chemicals he stored in his basement really opened my eyes. So we struck a deal. In return for letting him go, he taught me the kind of chemistry you just don't get to study in high school."

Piet listens with eyes wide and fearful. "This is insane," is all he can say.

"The harsh truth is that you're about to suffer an undignified and painful death," confirms Ramsay, and returns the vial to his pocket. "Then again, if you tell me what I need to know, I can offer you the *antidote*." In place of the vial, he draws out a plastic pill canister between his thumb and forefinger. "Prussian blue," he says. "Take one capsule with water, three times a day, for the next month. You'll be very ill, of course, but you'll live. It's kinda hard to acquire, so you really should start talking to me."

"Give me that!" Piet attempts to grab the canister, but he's too slow.

Samuel Ramsay sucks the air between his teeth. "Where is she? It's very simple."

The man's action has caused some heads to turn. Ramsay seems quite unconcerned and keeps his eyes locked on Piet.

"I don't know," Piet relents, wide-eyed with panic now. "She complained the guy she'd escaped with had a crazy plan. Said he intended to head home, even though she thought it was a dumb move."

"To England?" Ramsay sounds somewhat surprised. "Where in England?"

"She didn't say."

"Shame," he says, and pockets the pill canister. At the same time, the waiter appears with a basket of bread. He sets it down between the two men. If he's aware of tension between them, he doesn't show it.

"Give me the antidote," hisses Piet, as soon as the waiter is out of earshot.

"*Where* were they heading?" insists Ramsay, with venom in his voice this time.

Piet is visibly shaking now. He swallows uncomfortably, almost sobbing as he does so.

"Beth sold me just one bar. She offered me another, but I wouldn't take it. Those things are stamped with the Fort Knox seal. They're hot as hell. When she realized I couldn't be persuaded, she asked about the best way to smuggle it onto an aircraft. She wanted to know what kind of security procedures were in operation at Heathrow."

Hearing this, Samuel Ramsay fishes the canister from his pocket. He tosses it across the table and rises to his feet. "Start the medication immediately, and don't miss a single dose." As Piet scrambles to pop the lid, the bounty hunter drops two twenty-euro notes on the table. "Lunch is on me," is the last thing he says before leaving. "If you still have the appetite."

Alone at the table, Piet reaches for his glass to wash down the pill. Just before it reaches his lips, he curses under his breath and favors the water belonging to his departed guest. He closes his eyes and drains the glass. On finishing, he is startled to find that the chair across from him is occupied. He recognizes the woman sitting there as one of the diners. She has been conversing with an older man at a nearby table. Piet looks around, but her companion has vanished.

"Repeat everything you just told Samuel Ramsay," she tells him, with just a hint of an accent to match her Persian features. She is undoubtedly very beautiful, with dark golden eyes, painted lips, and sculpted cheekbones. Even so, there is undiluted malice in the look she shoots him. "Tell me every detail, or I'll leave you wishing that he hadn't given you that antidote."

15

I AWAKE JUST AFTER MIDDAY, FOUR HOURS BEFORE MY ALARM IS DUE to ring. I'm used to sleeping fitfully. It is just one more aspect of my life that has been shaped by our fugitive status.

With an afternoon to kill, and feeling somewhat unsettled after my conversation with Beth, I decide to visit my father. This is something I've done every other week or so since arriving here. Not that he is aware of my presence. I know full well he's being watched. I've read the application and the authorization to have his telephone tapped and his e-mails intercepted.

In some ways, I am relieved that they have chosen to assure Dad that I'm still helping with their investigation into the Fort Knox heist. They've even been cooking up correspondence from me. I've seen digital copies of handwritten letters in my name that tell him I am being treated just fine. In one I even suggest that I will land a security consultancy role with the U.S. military once the Fort Knox affair has been cleaned up. Read in sequence, the letters make it sound like I'm enjoying the trip of a lifetime. No letters make any mention of the detainment camp where I was held, let alone the horrors I witnessed that led to my escape. Although each one has even been artfully censored with marker pen, it isn't hard to work out that they want him to believe I am residing in the States somewhere. I should've been outraged, but I remind myself that it's in my best interest. If my father knew the truth and broke the silence he had been ordered to keep, it could compromise his safety *and* mine. For this reason, I have resisted the temptation to make contact. Instead I settle with simply being near him.

My former home is only fifty minutes away by train. I wouldn't dream of getting that close, of course. The risk of being recognized by neighbors and friends is too great. Instead I head for the park overlooked by the office where he works. Twice I've glimpsed him. Once at a window. Another time stepping out to his car with a colleague. On both occasions it brought a lump to my throat as well as a bitter taste to my mouth. He looks like my dad, but with his heart and soul ripped out. Even though he's functioning normally, he's too gaunt, too gray, too detached, and I know full well that this is all because of me.

Usually I don't see him, and today is a case in point. Still, just being there helps me to feel close. It also fires a certain determination, and that is just what I need before I seek out a nearby Internet café and prepare for the night shift ahead.

16

I FIND WILSON IN THE MONITORING ROOM. HE'S IN FRONT OF THE keyboard, mouse in one hand, gazing at the large screen in the center. Unlike all the screens surrounding it, which feed in from the CCTVs mounted throughout the building, this one displays a recruitment website.

"Job hunting," he says, scrolling through the adverts. "Willard authorized permission for me to look for work from here."

"That's good of him," I say thinly, taking the other seat now.

"Not that I qualify for much. I'm well aware that most employers are going to favor younger men like you."

I watch the screen with him for a moment and feel the need to break the silence. "Wilson, if there is anything I can do to help, just let me know, okay?"

Wilson scrolls through the ads for a moment longer, then collapses the screen to reveal his résumé underneath.

"Can you work miracles?"

As he speaks, I note movement on a monitor in the upper row. The camera is mounted above the balcony airlock. It offers a view along the length of the walkway. Two figures have just set out toward the atrium end. I recognize Willard. The other man is a mystery. Unlike the security director, he's dressed quite casually in jeans and a collarless, long-sleeved shirt.

"Who's that?" I ask.

Wilson looks up from his résumé. "That'll be one of Cleopatra's operators. The system administrator or one of the software guys. Hard to tell from behind. All geeks look alike, in my view."

"How many operators does she have?"

Wilson shrugs. "I don't pay so much attention to the technical personnel rota. Often it's a different face at the end of each day. All I know is that Cleo has a fully vetted team at her beck and call. The skill sets required are too numerous for an individual."

I watch the two men reach the airlock on the far side and disappear from the frame. Wilson offers to make the first tea of the shift. He leaves me watching every monitor rotate through a sequence of shots. All is still within Sphinx Cargo. From the balcony offices to the cargo floor, there is no sign of life. For a minute I watch the monitor cycling through the exterior cameras. One shot shows Willard Thorn bidding farewell to the tech guy, before the pair climb into their cars. The next time the shot comes around, the parking spaces are empty.

I sit back, a sense of tedium kicking in already, and wonder if perhaps Wilson might find his return to the outside world a blessing in disguise. By the time a cup is placed in front of me, I realize I am watching the feeds rotate without paying attention to them at all. I thank Wilson for the tea and then blink as I focus on another one of the monitors.

"Where is that?" I ask, suddenly aware that the cameras on this screen show an entirely unfamiliar part of the building. I see a long corridor with glass doors on each side and pipes running the length of the ceiling.

Wilson returns to his seat. "You don't have to worry about it," he says quite casually. "We're not required to patrol the lower level."

17

I HAVE TO FORCE MYSELF NOT TO LEAP ON THIS REVELATION. WHAT Wilson has just told me comes as a complete surprise. As cool as I can, I ask him if he's thought about anything other than security work. At the same time, I struggle to summon the architect's blueprint to my mind. Nowhere was there any mention of a subterranean floor. From what I had come across, the whole building had been designed to accommodate cargo on one level only.

"Night watch is what I know," says Wilson. "But hey, I haven't asked what draws a lad like you to the job."

I am staring at the screen when he says this. "Excuse me?"

"Willard tells me your girlfriend works close by. He says you want to see more of her. Must be serious."

Briefly, I peel my eyes away from the monitors. "Wilson, what does the lower level contain?"

He turns to face me, as if surprised by my curiosity. "You

don't need to worry about that," he says. "For health and safety reasons, only specialist personnel have access."

With my gaze drawn to the screen again, I watch camera feeds from different points of the level play out in turn. As well as shots from the corridor, I see rooms with freezer chests. When the screen cuts to one with a biohazard sign clearly visible on the glass, I grasp what I am looking at here.

"It's for storing dangerous goods, right?"

Wilson shrugs and turns back to the employment website on the central screen. "Everything from corrosive, toxic, and infectious substances, if the paperwork is in order, Sphinx can keep it safe and sound until transit takes place. Some of the stuff, the volatile materials, needs round-the-clock monitoring. That's where Cleopatra comes into her own. She can make any necessary adjustments to the environment to ensure that everything stays as it should."

I say nothing for a moment, just stare at the screen and wonder why on earth this would've been kept from the architect's blueprint.

"How do you access it?" I ask.

"I would imagine with fingers crossed." Wilson chuckles to himself, then turns around to face me. "The loading chamber can also operate as an elevator. Sphinx can't afford to have that kind of material enter the main area. Once booked in, it goes straight down. As far as we're concerned, it's out of sight and out of mind." He stops there, sighs to himself, and returns the browser to the default page. "Normally at this time I like to do the rounds and think about what I'm going to write," he says. "It's going to be tough breaking out of the routine."

Immediately I make room for him to exit. "Don't mind me," I say. "I'll just stay here and surf. My girlfriend's itching for a career change. Maybe I should have a look on her behalf."

"Have you been set up with a user account yet?" he asks, rising from his seat. I shake my head. Wilson grins and claps me on the shoulder. "Feel free to borrow mine for now, but don't go viewing the kind of websites that could mess up my references."

I tell him I'll just close it down once I've finished. As Wilson leaves I take the seat. I don't touch the keyboard, however. I just wait until I see him arrive on the balcony monitor. Then I turn my attention to the feed from the camera in the stairwell behind me. I watch it creep full circle and calculate that I have just over a minute to carry out the task at hand.

At the first opportunity, I reach for the mouse and sign out of Wilson's account. Inside the log-in screen that appears, I rattle out Sara Sinclair's name along with the password that I've confirmed she uses. Then I hover my finger over the enter key and hold my breath.

There is an element of risk with any hacking activity. No

matter how much groundwork has been covered, at some point you need to take a chance. Right now, avoiding any visual evidence is just one small step I can take in minimizing the possibility of detection. The rest is down to my faith in the way systems like this are run.

Generally, within a closed computer network it's possible to log on as a user from any terminal. Everyone inside the firewall has been fully vetted, after all. I'm well aware that making such an attempt from the control hub is a risk too far. Wilson himself had warned me not even to touch the keyboard in there. At the same time, he seemed quite relaxed about leaving me in front of this one.

With my eyes fixed to the screen, and no way back without knowing Wilson's password, I sink my finger onto the key.

The cursor turns. Then the background shuts down on me. I brace myself for alarms to sound. Instead I hear a chime accompany the appearance of a welcome screen.

On the monitors, Wilson has just stepped onto the cargo floor. I see his flashlight beam cutting between pallets. Meanwhile the revolving camera behind me has just arrived at the locker room. With no time to spare, I summon Sara's e-mail folder.

I'm looking for just one message. A quarantine report from the antivirus software.

On a daily basis, any networked organization can expect to be hit by all manner of worms and viruses. Generally, such malware arrives in the form of junk mail, cooked up by script kiddies getting to grips with writing code. Then again, not all attacks are carried out by mischief-making amateurs. A professional, such as a corporate blackmailer or data thief, can find ways to artfully dodge the antivirus filters. Indeed, it's quite possible to receive an e-mail from an apparently legitimate source, only to find it contains a payload tailor-made to bring the system to its knees.

In view of such a threat, should the antivirus software intercept a suspect e-mail or attachment not previously encountered, it is sectioned off for the attention of the recipient. Quite simply, it requires human judgment to make the call, so innocent communications don't get iced.

With a smile, I count half a dozen quarantine reports still unopened in Sara's inbox. More often than not, the suspect e-mails turn out to be junk. In some ways, it makes the reports an annoyance in their own right. That's why I had banked on her glancing at this one and moving on without taking action. Eventually, the e-mail on hold will be destroyed automatically, along with the attachment, so why bother going through the motions when the system does it for you?

On clicking through from the report to the quarantine folder, I find exactly what I'm looking for. An e-mail from a bogus account I'd set up. It contains two attachments. Simple programs I'd assembled myself over recent weeks. Earlier this afternoon, having given up hope of seeing my father, I'd logged in at an Internet café and sent off both to Sara.

"Well, hello!" I say under my breath, and select the option to release the e-mail into her in-box. She has many subfolders set up in there, and so I pocket it in one she hasn't opened in months. Finally, I mark it as read so it doesn't show up, close down the user session, and then hurriedly sit back from the keyboard.

On the security room monitor, I watch myself creep into the frame. Knowing this Trojan horse is in place, ready to open up at my bidding, I casually drink my tea while it's still hot.

18

I CHOOSE NOT TO TELL BETH STRAIGHTAWAY ABOUT THE PROGRESS I've made. Logging on from Wilson's terminal was an educated gamble. Even so, it left me stressed out for the rest of that shift. Whenever I walked under a camera, I felt certain Cleopatra had her attention locked on me. Was she biding her time? Waiting for me to make another move to back up her suspicions? I know I was being paranoid, but working in such a vast environment after dark was enough to set the mind racing.

Back at the flat, Beth and I eat from boxes of noodles we picked up at the airport. She seems quiet and reflective. I watch her twist her fork inside the box, eyes turned down.

"When you were little," she says, "what did you dream you would be?"

"Something involving computers," I reply after a moment. "I didn't really have a burning ambition."

She smiles to herself, a hint of sadness in her eyes.

"We're so different," she says. "Growing up on a farm sur-rounded by older brothers, I wanted to prove myself from an early age. More than anything, I wanted to show that nothing could hold me back."

I chew on my food, thinking about this. "Most girls I know haven't robbed Fort Knox, or escaped from a maximum-security military detention center," I point out. "You're doing good."

"I feel like I'm going nowhere," she replies, breathing out like this is some kind of confession. "I understand why you want to crack the system at Sphinx. I listen to you enthuse about Cleo-patra, and you're all lit up. I just hear you out, think about the bullion inside, and wonder what I'm doing. We've come this far by working together. Why can't we pool our skills and peel this tin can open?"

I set my fork down and push my noodles away.

"What if I said go ahead?" I ask. "How about I invite you to step inside Sphinx and help yourself to the bars? What would you do with them? Exactly how would you convert any of them into cash without attracting the attention of the people we're in hiding from?"

I realize I'm being sharp with her, but after a long night the last thing I need is this.

When Beth rises from the table, I think the conversation is closed. Instead she says, "You're at the top of your game, Carl. I'm at the top of mine. Remember the funds that got us here? I came up with a whole bunch of euros when we needed it most."

"And I'll always be grateful to you for that."

"Except you never asked me how I raised the money."

"I figured you stole it. You were lucky, Beth. I'm grateful for the break it gave us, but I don't operate like that."

"I made it by cashing in something valuable to me."

Looking up at her, seeing that wicked smile cross her face, I feel my stomach tighten.

"Oh no," I say, stunned when she nods. "One of the Fort Knox bars?"

"I didn't get a great deal for it, but then my contact knew I had no choice but to accept whatever he offered. I trusted him to keep his mouth shut, however. So under the circumstances it was a fair trade."

I sink my head into my hands. "Beth, do you realize what a risk you ran?"

"I sure do," she says, collecting the finished noodle boxes. "It gave me just the kind of kick you're enjoying at Sphinx."

Still reeling, I follow her into the kitchenette.

"We could've been tailed," I stress. "It could've put an end to everything."

"But it didn't," she said, dropping the boxes in the bin. "And if you want me to prove a point, I have the means to do it again."

She faces me now, nostrils flaring, and then heads out into the hallway.

I am left staring at the bin, struggling to work out what she means. A moment later I hear a thumping sound from the bathroom. When I find her, Beth is on her knees with the paneling from under the sink in her hands. That's when I see the object stashed under the pipes. It's wrapped in a towel, which she gathers with both hands and sets on her lap.

"Oh, Beth," I say, lost for words as she peels back the towel, one fold at a time. "What have you done?"

In these surroundings, a domestic bathroom with damp and mildew in every crevice and corner, a gold bullion bar looks totally out of place.

"If we ever need to vanish in a hurry," she says, "this will pay the way."

I can't believe that she's done this. I think back to the fact that we weren't even in the country when she took off to make this trade. It means she must have smuggled the bar with her when we flew in under false names.

"You're crazy," I say, feeling both shock and rising anger now. "What were you thinking? We could've been picked up by customs at any point."

"Which made me feel *so* alive," she says. "And now we have an opportunity to make *millions* from Sphinx!"

The way she holds my gaze makes it completely clear how much this means to her. The temperature between us is climbing, but I don't have the will to push it higher.

"Beth—"

"I could've cashed in this bar at any time," she cuts in, and wraps it back inside the towel. "All I ask is that you think things through, Carl. I know your focus is on cracking Cleopatra, but why waste the opportunity to clean up at the same time?"

19

WHEN I ARRIVE FOR WORK, FOUR SHIFTS INTO MY NEW POST, I KNOW just what Sara is going to tell me.

"You're on your own tonight. Can you believe Wilson has been approached about a new job? He didn't even apply! Apparently the airport bus depot people are looking to hire a night watch. They heard he's about to become available and think he fits the bill."

"Are they interviewing?" I ask, despite the fact that I set it all up in advance. A virtual visit to the employment agency had enabled me to add Wilson's details to the database. I then pinpointed what looked like an ideal post for him and put in the call. Speaking as an agency representative, I sold the guy to the depot with such confidence that they agreed to see him at the earliest opportunity.

"He came by this afternoon to tell me," Sara says, preparing to leave for the day as usual. "He looked a treat in his suit, even if I did have to straighten out his tie."

"I'm sure you sent him off looking like a million dollars," I say. "Wilson's done a great job bringing me up to speed here. I reckon I'll be fine on my own tonight."

On turning to head up the open stairs, I note Willard Thorn stepping out of the airlock. He brushes down his lapel, as if perhaps a speck of dust has inexplicably escaped extraction. "Young man," he announces, which causes my heart to skip a beat. "I've caught you at last."

I climb the steps to meet him and tell myself to stay calm. "Is there a problem, sir?"

From the top of the staircase, the security director regards me with both hands behind his back. "I think we both know the answer to that."

I meet his eyes and keep on advancing as if nothing is wrong.

"Wilson told me you used his log-in," he says, and steps aside as I come close. "You really should have your own, and I apologize for not doing it sooner."

He extends his hand as I reach the top. Smiling, I shake it heartily. "That's great news," I say, for it sounds to me like he's just made my position permanent. "I won't let you down."

"No, you won't," he replies, and though he flashes me a grin, it sounds like an order. "I hear you're flying solo tonight. Good luck with that."

"With Cleopatra at the controls," I say, and this time it is my turn to smile, "we're in safe hands until sunrise."

On my first tour of the main floor, I find a barbecued rat. I shine my flashlight into the overhead vaults, aware of the firepower within these walls and the sensors trained on me. I still don't feel as if I have fully earned the trust of the supercomputer that has me under her observation. Still, before dawn breaks I intend to have secured that for sure.

Wilson showed me where to deposit the vermin. I take the corpse to the chute beside the airlock, drop it in, and close the hatch. It reminds me of the lower level beneath my feet and what I have to do before I can investigate further.

On my return to the monitoring room, I ignore every camera swiveling in my wake. I even brew myself a cup of coffee without once showing an awareness of the slow-turning lens in the stairwell. It's only when I'm stationed in my chair that I focus my attention on the feed from the camera behind me. I swig my drink, counting down the moments until I am out of the picture. Then I log on in Sara's name.

My e-mail is still hidden away inside the subfolder. With one click I open it up and execute the first of the two file attachments. For a few seconds nothing happens. My heart begins to pound. I catch my breath when the screen shudders. At the same

111

moment, the surrounding monitors switch to white static and the low lights dip throughout the building. Thanks to the crippling virus I have just uploaded, I even hear the revolving camera stop dead.

Cleopatra may be physically immune to attack from the outside. From within, as I have just proven, she is as vulnerable as any other system.

"Okay," I say, speaking freely to myself now. "Let's go to work."

I bring up the command screen and summon a list of all the directories on the network. The one belonging to the system administrator is my target, and when I open it up I find just what I'm looking for: the user name database for Sphinx Cargo's personnel. Without pause for thought, I reset all passwords. The system accepts my request. I am now free to log on as anyone I choose.

Before I do so, however, I feel it is only right that I am sitting at the heart of the operation.

20

I STAND BEFORE THE BRUSHED-STEEL PYRAMID FEELING VERY TENSE
indeed. Every camera I passed on the way up remained stationary.
I feel like I am responsible for incapacitating some venerated
god. There is no way back from here. I have come this far. All I
can do now is take things to the next stage.

"Cleo," I say, addressing the pyramid, "I know your sensors are
idle right now. Otherwise, every alarm in the building would be
ringing. Let me just say I mean you no harm. I want to be friends.
I hope in a moment we'll have a long-lasting connection."

I take to the high-backed chair and draw myself closer to the
desk. Like every monitor inside Sphinx Cargo at this time, the
two screens before me show exactly the same basic command
screen that I had run from the monitoring room.

From the keyboard, I raise the log-in fields. Next, having
made a note of it before leaving the monitoring room, I enter
the system administrator's user name. There is no need to enter

a password. On hitting enter, many sequential lights blink and flutter within the pyramid. I watch the monitors with a catch in my throat. It is only when the welcome screen appears that I know for sure that I am well and truly in.

I am fully aware that I now have full command of Cleopatra. I also know that it is going to take me a long while to work out how to communicate with a supercomputer—and now is not the time. Instead I move quickly to set up a new user account. It's a simple task. I call it "Test" for the sake of a name that sounds both routine and anonymous should it ever be discovered. I then copy over all the permissions and privileges from the account I am working from. Finally, I render it invisible within the user name directory. In effect, I have created a secret replica key. One that gives me total access during the hours of darkness.

"You'll be pleased to know the operation has been a complete success," I tell Cleopatra, having signed out of the system. "Once I run the recovery program, you'll come round feeling just fine. The only difference will be the additional account I've just set up for myself and nicely tucked away. So, if you'll excuse me, I'll complete the procedure from my own workstation. I wouldn't want you to find me in the hot seat, after all."

As I leave the control hub, I feel the kind of euphoria I enjoyed on opening the vault at Fort Knox. Now that I'm able to open the door without alarms sounding, I even sneak a peek inside the third and final stairwell at the opposite end of the gallery. I may not be hacking for fun anymore, but nothing beats the buzz of knowing I have beaten a system. All I do is peer into the gloom, hear the backup generator humming, and then remind myself that I still have work to do.

On my return to the opposite side of the balcony, I practically dance down the spiral staircase. It's only when I reach the final turn that I stop abruptly.

At first I think I have imagined that the swivel camera just lurched into life by several degrees. I stare at the device, aware that the lens is attempting to pull focus, and gasp when it moves again. This time, the faltering action begins to smooth out. I can barely believe what this means and race for the monitoring room before I am caught in its field of vision.

I had customized the virus myself. The creator was some Russian script kiddie hoping to freeze his college server for a time so he could amend his records. I had picked it up from a hackers' bulletin board. The code was full of errors, of course, all of which I tidied up, but above all I liked the fact that it wasn't intended to cause damage. More important, it came with a recovery program. Not only did this immediately release the system from paralysis, it restored all vital functions to a point exactly sixty seconds *before* the virus had struck.

That Cleopatra appears to be stirring just tells me just what kind of processor power I'm up against here. Even in a deep coma, it seems she is struggling to revive herself. Should she surface by her own accord, I've no doubt that she'll consider my actions a very hostile threat indeed.

"Don't mess up now," I mutter, throwing myself into the chair. Punching in Sara's log-in details, I access her e-mail account and fire up the second attachment. This time, to my horror, Cleopatra fails to respond as planned. The screen glitches, but the CCTV monitors continue to feed through static.

"No, no, *no*!"

Seized by panic, I shut down Sara's account and wheel around in the chair. I'm ready to run, overwhelmed by a need to bail if I can, and find myself looking directly into the eye of the camera. At first it appears to have locked on me, only to begin revolving smoothly as if nothing unusual has happened.

Without blinking I watch it turn, the motor ticking over quietly, before snapping to face the monitors once more. This time, I see every feed back up and running. I breathe out long and hard. After a brief delay, I realize Cleopatra has at last come round as I intended. She may have lost a minute, approaching midnight now, but that will be corrected automatically. I know she won't reject the new account I have implanted, though all I can do is pray there are no side effects.

With a sigh of relief, I flop back into my chair. My brow is

beaded with sweat—and not just because the air and temperature controls have been idle for a short while. I reach for the keyboard once more, preparing to log on now with all the privileges
of the system administrator. This time I smile to myself in relief
as much as anticipation.

For all is well on my watch, and by the time the clock strikes,
things can only get better.

21

ONCE I HAVE ASSUMED CONTROL OF CLEOPATRA, IT'S SAFE FOR ME to leave the monitoring room. This time the cameras follow me, but I'm not regarded as a threat. I am simply the night watch. The guy hired to please the clients when they ask who is present through the nocturnal hours.

As far as the system is concerned, I am also someone with every right to quietly call the shots.

"Shall we begin?" I ask, on settling into the seat back in the control hub. One screen shows my location within the building, signified by a blinking green dot. The other awaits my first line of command. "If we're going to have a relationship, Cleo, clear communication is vital."

I settle my fingers over the keyboard, only to pause when a thought enters my head. Inside this metal box, on a crummy trading estate, I realize I have accessed the kind of technology that most hackers would kill to get their hands on.

As I close my hand around the mouse, I feel like I'm breaking new ground. The command options are easy to find, even if they are numerous. Cleopatra might possess capabilities that have already exceeded my expectations, but the system administrator set her up to drive like a dream. I study the list, arranged in sections, and wonder where to begin.

"Synchronize cranes," I say out loud. I click on the command, feeling goofy all of a sudden. Whatever I have just engaged, it sounds like the kind of thing some evil genius would declare.

The hum of machinery powering up from the main floor draws me to the balcony. I look out through the glass, just as hundreds of grab hooks descend from the gloom. I watch them open up like flowers in fast motion. When they spin, I laugh out loud. It's as if they're performing for me, before bowing out by retracting as one. I realize I've simply asked the system to align the cranes, but the kick is overwhelming.

I cannot wait to get back into the seat to find out what else I can ask her to do.

"Soundtrack?" I say to myself, questioning why such a command would be there. I have no intention of filling the space with pulsing electronica, but that's exactly what happens when I test it out. My instinct is to shut it down. Then I remember how the shell of the building had all but insulated the roar of the planes. I note that some of the lights within the pyramid are beating in time to the track, and decide to enjoy what is evidently a little off-the-record programming on the part of the system administrator.

Half an hour later, wearing my face mask and oxygen backpack, I stand on the walkway overlooking the cargo floor. With my hands on the rails I am nodding to the music, while all around me the lights flash and strobe. Having discovered how to make the electroshock cannons fire tracers instead of needles, I watch harmless phosphorus bolts shoot out from underneath the gantry. The moving targets in their sights are also under my control. With every crane crisscrossing the space, the grab claws gliding between pallets at right angles to one another, I realize I am witnessing one hell of a spectacle.

In some ways, it's a celebration. A private moment for myself. Because from here on out the hard work begins. Despite the apparent chaos I have caused, I am entirely confident that Cleopatra has not placed the cargo at any risk. The instinct to protect is hardwired into her system, as I can see with my own eyes.

From my next shift onward, my goal is to have her extend that level of protection to Beth and me in the outside world.

22

PASSPORT CONTROL, TERMINAL 4, HEATHROW AIRPORT, UK

THE BOUNTY HUNTER STANDS BEFORE THE OFFICER IN THE RAISED booth. His face is impassive, as it is on the carefully constructed document he's just handed over. In the picture his hair is a little less gray, combed to one side, and with only the beginnings of a beard. He may have even gained a few pounds since then, but it's undeniably the same guy in the picture. Samuel Ramsay has no reason to be nervous. As the passport was quietly issued to him by his CIA contacts, it's as legitimate as those belonging to the chattering party of tourists behind him.

"Thank you, sir," says the officer, returning the passport. "Have a pleasant stay."

Ramsay travels light. With only a canvas sports bag slung across his back, he walks briskly around the luggage carousel toward the Arrivals hall. It's been some time since he carried a weapon. Even then, the gun belonged to his victim. Of course, he has access to firepower that can be broken down into parts guaranteed to pass without suspicion through any X-ray machine. It just isn't how he's operated since he lost his CIA badge. In the past decade, Ramsay has schooled himself in alternative methods of persuasion and killing. It means he can travel at a moment's notice.

So long as the price is right.

It's been quite a while since he has flown into Heathrow. On the last occasion, waiting for a connecting flight to Washington, D.C., the whiny guy he was bringing home had spent the whole time pleading his innocence. He doesn't remember the details. Some corporate fraudster who had skipped bail and then the country. Whatever excuses he had given, Ramsay was wise to them all. Back then, the bounty hunter had shepherded him into the restroom and punched him repeatedly in the kidneys until he promised to zip it for the rest of the journey.

Striding through the hall now, he finds the airport is still the overcrowded and slightly chaotic people farm that it's always been. The only difference is the endless bleating from cell phones. Ramsay joins the shortest queue he can find at a bureau de change. It's late in the day, and the sooner he has the necessary cash, the quicker he can check into a nearby hotel. From there, it will just be a question of visiting the handful of known bullion smugglers and launderers within the UK and making it quite clear where their allegiance should lie. If Beth Nelson has smuggled in a gold bar, it will only be a matter of time before she breaks her cover in order to convert it. Even if that doesn't lead directly to the hacker, Ramsay will at least have the means to draw him into the open.

At the cashier's window, Ramsay waits patiently as the transaction is carried out. Watching the woman behind the glass count the money, he pays no attention to the hum of activity behind him. Not even the perfume-counter girl and the young guy dropping her off for another night shift.

23

"GUESS WHAT?"

Wilson is waiting for me when the airlock opens. I have just crossed the walkway, wondering whether anything might be out of place. It looks absolutely fine to me. After last night's display, I watched Cleopatra retract every crane and dampen down the lights. Even so, I cannot shake off the fear that I'm playing with fire here.

"Did I forget to wash my coffee cup?" I step out of the airlock and face him with a grin. "Sara just told me you got the interview," I say in all seriousness. "How did it go?"

"Couldn't have been better," he says. "I really think they like me."

Together we head for the monitoring room.

"When will you find out?" I ask.

"Very soon, so they said. I really think it's in the bag. I just don't understand how they found out I was looking for employment."

I hold the door open for Wilson. "People keep their ears to the ground, I guess."

Wilson pauses at the top of the spiral staircase. "Here's the thing." He turns to face me. "An employment agency recommended me. The same one put you forward for this job."

"Is that so?" I shrug and encourage him to keep moving. Wilson doesn't budge. He regards me now, half smiling.

"You wouldn't have had anything to do with that, would you?" He holds my gaze, forcing me to think on my feet.

"Okay," I say. "I might have put in a good word to the guys there. I've worked for them for some time. They trust my judgment."

Wilson nods to himself and then extends his hand. "Thank you, man. I haven't known you for long, but Sphinx is lucky to have you here."

At the foot of the stairwell, I volunteer to put the kettle on. As I do so, I hear Wilson ease into his chair. I feel good about what I've done for him, even if it served my own purposes. It also brings a little relief from the nagging feeling that Beth and I are beginning to drift. On our escape from Camp Twilight, it really did seem like the world was against us. Every hardship we faced just brought us closer together. Now, hiding out here near the airport, I sense that Beth has run out of patience. Part of me wants to walk out now and assure her that I am working hard to secure our freedom. What stops me is the continued belief that my actions could speak louder than words.

"Hey, Wilson," I say, bringing him a mug of tea. "Let me make the first round of the evening. I could do with stretching my legs."

"Fine by me." Wilson is sitting in front of his manuscript, leafing through the pages. "If you disturb any vermin, just stand well back."

I find no rats on my inspection of the main floor. Instead, every time I sweep my flashlight beam across the path, I see nothing but gold ingots. It's as if they've conspired to catch the light and remind me of the one thing guaranteed to keep Beth onside.

"No way," I tell myself at one point and switch the beam elsewhere. "That isn't why I'm doing this."

I spend a long time roaming this labyrinth of treasures. I'm just not ready to return and make idle conversation. In navigating this vast maze, I begin to recognize certain sculptures and artworks. Toward the center, one pallet is laden with African tribal artifacts, another with diamond trays. Three blocks behind, I know I'll find a cage containing rocks and boulders. Closer inspection reveals glittering seams. It's a precious metal of some description, waiting to be broken out and valued. Despite such distractions, I can't shake off my anxiety about Beth. At one point, on crossing beneath the overhead walkway, I'm so lost in thought that the sound of an electroshock cannon swiveling causes me to jump out of my skin.

I aim my flashlight beam higher, alarmed to find not just one but all the cannons aiming directly at me.

"Hey, hold on!" I say, freezing on the spot. "It's me!" Carefully, I take a step backward. Every cannon follows my position by differing degrees. I keep retreating until I can duck behind a pallet. There, with my back to a crate, I struggle to hold my nerve. *What's going on?* I ask myself. *What is happening here?*

The shock leaves me struggling to make sense of the situation. All I know is that suddenly, and for no apparent reason, Cleopatra regards me as a threat.

With my heart in my mouth, I leave my hiding place and head for the airlock. I am aware that at any time several cannons will have me in their sights, and yet not a single needle is fired. I keep walking, the sound of my breathing amplified by the headgear. "Don't shoot," I say under my breath. "Don't shoot. Don't shoot."

On clearing the final pallet, I break for the airlock. I know I shouldn't panic, but I have seen what those weapons can do. I scramble to open the door, thinking perhaps this is some kind of payback for compromising the system, and throw myself inside. The door slides shut. I rip off my breathing apparatus as soon as

I am able and take a gulp of air. In the bright light, as the airlock opens up on the other side, I wonder if I have just suffered a panic attack.

Upstairs, I peer through the darkened glass of the control hub. The room is empty. On making my way along the corridor, I'm aware that the security cameras are following me. While this is to be expected, I hadn't anticipated coming under computer-controlled crosshairs. I still feel rattled as I head down the spiral staircase, but also increasingly irritated. I feel sure that somehow Wilson must be behind it. A prank, perhaps, designed to shake me up. Then I find him in the monitoring room, snoring in his seat. Only then do I realize the man has no idea of the grief he's responsible for just triggering.

24

AS SOON AS SHE DETECTED THAT WILSON WAS ASLEEP ON THE JOB, Cleopatra had gone into a state of alert. The way I see things, the sensors that picked up on his motionless form had fed through the system. As a precaution, the cannons then took to tracking the only other human presence in the building.

I stand over him now, wondering what I should do.

"Hey, buddy, wake up," I say, but don't have the heart to push it. The guy is slumped over the desk, embracing his manuscript as if it's a pillow.

Instead, thinking on my feet, I decide to use this moment to my advantage.

Mindful of the camera revolving behind me, I choose my moment to lean over the guard I'm here to replace and log him off the system. I then sign on as Cleopatra's special guest. Immediately, a status report scrolls up the screen. It informs me of the security lapse, logging the time to the tenth of a second.

"Aww, he doesn't deserve this trouble." Quietly, I find the instruction to cancel the alert. As Cleo stands down, I go on to delete the report. For both our sakes, I don't want the directors of Sphinx Cargo to be made aware of this slip-up. Wilson deserves to enjoy his last shifts here, just as I need the time and space to myself. As far as I am concerned, he can sleep until sunrise.

Switching off the central monitor now, I leave Wilson to his slumbers and head for the stairwell.

Tonight, as I take my seat before this magnificent pyramid, I have no intention of asking Cleo to put on a show. What I'm looking to understand is how she connects with the outside world. Physically, I'm well aware of the steps that have been laid out to keep this building secure. For all the measures taken, however, there has to be an access point for the virtual flow of information. Every staff member has an e-mail account and access to the Internet, while I figure a freight outfit like this would need some kind of link to real-time flight schedules at the very least.

"List all ports," I say to myself, clicking on what reads like the right command.

Immediately, on the other screen I am surprised to be presented with a wireframe view of the building. It swivels on an invisible axis to show a top-down perspective, and then appears to sprout fast-moving vines around the entire structure. Within a moment it's entirely enveloped and shows just one cable connecting Sphinx to the surrounding telecommunications network.

"Amazing," is all I can say, and even then it comes out in a whisper. "You really *are* built to survive."

In awe, I realize that the whole building has been rigged up like some kind of giant antenna. I take in my surroundings once more. This time I'm aware that every square foot of the outside shell, the supporting walls, and even the foundations, contain powerful transmitter and receiver technology. According to the details, should the company's hardwire Internet access ever go offline, the system could simply hijack a wireless connection via anything from a wifi hotspot at the airport to one of the many communication satellites that continually orbit the globe. The reach, according to the information at my fingertips, extends upward and outward by a radius of fifty miles.

With the solar-powered backup generator tucked away inside the building, the surrounding landscape outside could be laid to waste and Cleopatra would *still* function normally. In terms of the technology in position to protect her cargo, this place leaves Fort Knox looking like a prehistoric cave.

"Okay, Cleo, let me teach you some hacking principles. Your first move is *reconnaissance*." As I speak I find the search facility and watch the screen change accordingly.

This is no standard search engine, however. I cannot afford

to seek out information about Beth and me like that. Without doubt, the authorities would have a virtual wiretap set up across the Web for any such request. What I have here, I realize, is a limitless army of Web crawlers. By dispatching these byte-sized, self-generating technological spiders, every corner of the Internet can be continually monitored for any mention of our names.

Looking at the code behind these crawlers, summoned at a keystroke, I realize I can encourage them one step further. Of course I'm keen to see what has been written about us on the Internet. More importantly, I want to know about any *communications*. Now or at any time in the future. This can't be achieved by monitoring websites. It has to come from bugging servers: those computers at the gateway of any organization that send and receive files, e-mails, and instant messages.

The task I have in mind is immense, for billions of servers all over the globe are plugged into the World Wide Web. For a supercomputer like this one, capable of continually generating my modified crawlers, it's as simple as running a screensaver.

Having tweaked the code, I hit the dispatch button. On the left-hand screen, I watch a visual representation of my crawlers stream into the network and punch the air in delight.

"Fly, my pretties!" I chuckle to myself. "Let's show who's in charge here."

It's only when I settle back in my chair that I realize I'm not alone.

"What's going on?" A voice from the doorway. I spin around and find Wilson looking rumpled and confused. "Son, what in hell are you doing?"

25

FOR A BEAT I SAY NOTHING. IN THAT MOMENT I SEE ALL MY EFFORTS TO keep Beth and myself at liberty have been ruined. I rise to my feet, a croak in my voice as I struggle to cover why I'm here in the hub.

"It isn't what you think."

I say this because I *have* to offer him something. Operating behind a screen or over the phone, I know that I can spin a tale out of nothing. Here, face-to-face with someone I have grown to like, I am lost for words.

Wilson throws his hands wide. "So what am I thinking?" he asks, sounding on the verge of anger now. "I know what I'm looking at. I just don't understand why Cleo hasn't sounded every alarm in the building!"

He comes closer, clearly still struggling with what he has found. Standing here, I'm half wondering if I should just run.

"You were sleeping," I say uselessly. "I didn't want to wake you."

"Evidently." Wilson glances over his shoulder at the pyramid and then returns his attention to me. "Last time I nodded off, she blasted a siren to stir me."

"I disabled it before that could happen."

As soon as I say this, some surprise comes into his expression. It reflects exactly how I'm feeling. I can barely believe that I have told him the truth, but there is no way now that I can take it back.

"You can do that?" he asks.

Looking at the keyboard, it seems I have no choice now but to take a gamble. I barely know the guy, but fleeing now would bring even more trouble crashing down on me.

"I can do a lot of things," I tell him, thinking that just perhaps I have earned his trust, "if you'll just give me a chance to explain myself."

Wilson holds my gaze, as if seeking to find some explanation simply from the look on my face.

"I should be summoning Thorn," he says, too quietly for me to feel comfortable. "What's to stop me from doing that?"

"I'm not here to rob the place. I swear."

Wilson breathes in and then shakes his head with a sigh.

"This is *bull*!" he says, with some anger returning. "I'm making that call."

"Please! Just hear me out!" Overcome by desperation and panic, I'm on my feet as he reaches for the phone on the desk. I barely register what has just left my lips, but it's enough for him to stop in his tracks. "All I ask is that you give me a moment of your time."

Immediately, I realize I have never put into words the account of what has happened to me. I know I should spin him a cover story, but I am also struck by a sudden need to unload the truth. Whether it's the shock of being caught red-handed, or my gut instinct that Wilson won't betray me, I feel no need to manipulate what I have to say here. From the moment the men in black pulled up beside me on my way home from college one afternoon, I have simply lived each moment as it comes. Suddenly it all feels like too much to carry inside. I realize it's also going to sound like the story of someone else's life, which causes me to hesitate.

"Go on," says Wilson eventually. "There's clearly more to you than meets the eye."

To his credit, over the next half an hour, Wilson does not interrupt me. He allows me to explain how an apparently casual dare to virtually open the Fort Knox vault led me to be locked up in an icebound detainment camp for America's most wanted mercenaries. I tell him that this is where I first met Beth and learned that she had masterminded the robbery that earned me all this trouble. Even when I detail why we had no choice but to escape during a botched and bloody uprising, he simply hears me out, nodding on occasion, and it comes as such a relief to put it all into words. I even share my fears about the lack of justice I encountered throughout, how it forced me to adopt a false identity, and why I no longer believe that it is in my best interests to turn myself in. Finally, when I outline my hope to enroll Cleopatra in my bid to stay ahead of the game, he runs his hand to the nape of his neck and simply stares at me.

The last thing I expect him to do, however, is laugh. It starts as a chuckle, like a response to some internal joke, but within moments I am facing a man who cannot control his amusement.

"Whatever next?" he asks, struggling to find the words. "Did you uncover a military conspiracy about alien contact?"

"I'm sorry?" I say, taken aback. "You don't believe me?"

"Tell it to the judge," he replies, recovering now. "If it amuses the court as it amuses me, they might cut your jail time."

When he moves to put in the call once more, I don't simply rise from my seat. This time, I sweep the phone from his reach. Having bared my heart and soul, I am not prepared to give in just like that. "I can't prove any of it to you," I say, shaking now, "but I swear on my life that I'm no thief. The only thing I'm here to steal is a small space inside Cleopatra's operating system, just so I can stay out of trouble. I'm a hacker, Wilson, but I'm no threat. Computer systems are so central to our security nowadays that anyone who takes an interest in how they work makes the people in charge feel deeply paranoid."

"Maybe for good reason," Wilson grumbles, and for a moment the tension between us brings only silence.

"So turn me in." I pause there, collect the phone from the floor, and hand it to Wilson. "Make that call and watch them come for me. The scale of the operation will be overwhelming. All for the kid you see here. Of course, they'll make you sign all kinds of papers guaranteeing your silence, and you'll never see or hear from me again. Quite literally, they'll spirit me away."

Wilson flattens his lips and lifts his attention from the phone.

"The job I just landed," he says, "when the agency called to put me forward for the interview, they claimed I'd been on their computer database for some time. Now, I'm smart enough to keep my mouth shut. I need the work, after all. But would you know something about that as well? I figured all you'd done was have a word. I'm thinking now you might've taken things further."

I look to the floor and nod. "I was just trying to do the right thing."

"So it seems," replies Wilson. I find him grinning at me.

"Damn it, boy. This is the most *intense* thing I ever heard!"

I take a moment to digest this. "So you won't say anything?"

"And risk throwing away my new job?" He waves away the suggestion. "If you can give me your word that you're not here to rob the joint, that's good enough for me."

I close my eyes and breathe. "I can't tell you what this means," I say, overcome with relief. "If there's anything I can do . . ."

"Hey," he says, stabbing a finger at me now. "You already did. Unless you can fix it for me to clean up at the bookmakers, I'll settle for the post at the bus depot."

It's only when his expression turns to concern that I realize my eyes have begun to shine.

"I'm okay," I say, and furiously wipe at the tears with my sleeve. "It's been a long time coming, I guess."

At this, Wilson looks as awkward as I feel. "I'm going to fix us some coffee," he says. "When I come back, I want to watch you go to work. I guess your actions will speak louder than words. But hear me now, Carl, if you're conning me, I'll be onto you."

"No problem," I say, smiling as I recover my composure. For I realize that had I tried to sell this man a story, he might well have failed to buy it. "It'll be good to have the company."

Wilson nods and retreats to the door once more. There, he considers me one final time. "How old are you again, son?"

"Eighteen," I say.

Wilson nods, digesting this, it seems. "I wasn't much older than you when I went to war," he tells me. "Watch out for yourself, do you hear?"

26

I DECIDE NOT TO TELL BETH ABOUT WILSON. HAVING UNMASKED MYSELF to him, I leave work with mixed feelings. All I can think is that he caught me entirely off guard. That's why it all spilled out. My gut instinct is that he will not betray me. Even so, I can't help thinking that informing Beth would only risk the temperature between us rising higher still. Instead, when I head out to the airport, I plan to update her on all the progress I have made with Cleopatra.

With Wilson at my side, I watched the first Web crawlers return. These front-runners had collected the easy stuff. Information about me in the public domain. According to their reports, my disappearance hadn't made headlines. I didn't take it personally, however. The posting supposedly from myself on the social networking site I once used spoke volumes. For it announced that I had dropped out of college to go traveling and that I'd be back in due course. Way back when the men in black first came for me, my father had been advised to adopt the same story. For his sake, I just hope he still believes that staying silent remains in the best interest of his son.

"These guys really don't want you causing trouble for them," Wilson remarked as we finished reading the thread.

"It's too late for that now," I replied, feeling all fired up once again. "And from here on out I'm raising the stakes."

Feeling stung by what I'd found, I located the program that effectively taught Cleopatra new tricks. Having shown her how to undertake a reconnaissance exercise, I wanted to continue equipping this supercomputer with the hacking skills to keep us from being hunted down. By referring to the range of instructions already logged in her system, I began bolting together additional rules and tasks for her to undertake.

My objective was simple, one Cleopatra was already programmed to understand. I simply wanted to add my name and Beth's to the list of cargo she should monitor and protect.

The threats, when they arose, would be picked up by Cleo from the Web crawlers' reports. On discovering any mention of Beth or myself, dispatched in an e-mail or attached document, I showed her how to *probe* the recipient's server for weaknesses, *access* it, and *advance* onto a user account so she could go to work. Once there, she was free to choose from a range of actions. Having made a copy for my attention, and dispatched it to an encrypted e-mail account, she was free to wipe the correspondence completely, substitute our names at random, or change any timings and locations.

As for the system from which the information originated, I instructed her how to bring it to its knees with one of the most basic and malevolent acts of hacking: a Denial of Service attack. Quite simply, if she felt the threat was sufficient, Cleopatra could flood the system with a stream of external data requests. It would be the equivalent of bombarding a phone with endless calls so that nobody could get a line in or out. The only way to deal with that was to pull the plug and start all over again.

In theory, and after months of preparation, I am putting the perfect plan into practice. In reality, having taken the first steps, I am left feeling increasingly unsettled about placing such trust in a supercomputer. Despite my belief in technology, I remind myself that I am just human.

If I completed my shift feeling rattled, what I find at the airport terminal leaves me close to panic. On approaching the perfume counter, I realize Beth is nowhere to be seen. Only her colleague is at the counter, in a pressed white lab coat and a deep fake tan.

"I've been on my own for an hour," she tells me as I cut through the drifting throng. "I'm surprised she didn't call."

"Did she say where she was going?" I ask, ignoring the

comment about the phone. Even as I speak I feel tension in my chest. We don't dare possess mobiles for fear of being bugged. As a result, since sneaking back into the country, Beth and I have made every effort to inform each other of our whereabouts. At any one time I know where she is and she knows the same about me. When her colleague shrugs at me, I turn on my heels as casually as I can and head directly for the exit.

It is only at the tower block, when the elevator fails to return to the ground floor, that I take the stairs at a sprint.

"Hey, there!" says Beth, as I crash through the door. She's just crossing from the bedroom to the kitchenette as I enter, tying back her hair at the same time. "You startled me!"

Breathlessly, I stare at her. "You weren't at work," I say. "Is something wrong?"

Without taking her eyes away, as if faced with a dangerous animal, she lowers her hands to her side. I glance over her shoulder. The bathroom door is ajar.

"Nothing is wrong," she says eventually, "but this feels like the right thing to do."

Solemnly, she invites me to follow her into the front room.

The cardboard box we use as a coffee table is draped in a throw, with a candle centerpiece burning in a jam jar. I look at the two dinner places, carefully laid out, but I have no appetite now.

"What's going on?" I ask, feeling numb all of a sudden. I turn to find her watching me from the doorway. "This feels like some kind of Last Supper!"

With a sigh, Beth invites me to take a seat.

HARE MARSH ARCHES, EAST LONDON, UK, THREE HOURS EARLIER

THE TRAINS RUN ON A HIGH-LEVEL LINE HERE, TRAVELING IN AND OUT of the capital. Underneath, the brick arches are tagged with graffiti and host to aggressive-looking weeds. They're also open for business, for this is where the black cabs come for repairs and servicing. On the forecourts, and inside these dim caverns, the vehicles can be seen jacked up in states of disassembly.

The bounty hunter crosses the road with a purpose. It's an overcast and blustery afternoon. He's wearing his anorak, zipped up halfway, and carries a small cardboard box. One of the mechanics looks up from under a hood as he approaches. At the same time, a train clatters overhead, drowning out the noise of the radio and several idling engines. The mechanic nods, in response to a question from this visitor, and points at a door plastered in stickers for tire and exhaust manufacturers.

Inside, Samuel Ramsay finds a man filling out forms at a desk. He's at work under a pool of light from an overhead lamp. It shines on his brow, but his face is cast in shadow.

"Boy, there's a storm in the air," says Ramsay, addressing the imposing figure of this 225-pound Bulgarian. "Good to see you, Stephan."

The guy in question, an East European émigré, looks up and immediately reaches for a drawer. For someone who runs an engine-tuning business, he seems unusually jumpy. But Stephan Mocet uses it as a front for a small-scale bullion-laundering operation, and the pistol he withdraws is a tool of the trade.

Ramsay seems unconcerned by the appearance of the weapon. He crosses the worn, grubby carpet, places the cardboard box on the desk, and spreads his hands.

"How long has it been?" he asks. "Five, six years?"

"Not long enough." Stephan eyes the box, the gun tight in his hand. The last time he encountered Ramsay, the man was in the pay of the CIA. Even then, on quizzing Mocet about an associate, he hadn't played entirely by the book. "If you're here to knock me unconscious again, perhaps this time you'll show me how you do it without leaving a mark. It's a useful technique."

"I'm not going to hurt you, Stephan. Relax."

"Then what *do* you want, scumbag?"

"Information," he tells him. "And a little respect."

"I'll offer you one if I can, but not the other."

Ramsay smiles and asks him about Beth Nelson. "She's back in town, with a bar to sell."

"From the Fort Knox job? That's too hot for me."

"Sure it is, Stephan. Has she been in touch?"

Stephan Mocet shakes his head, looking less anxious now. "If she does, you'll be the first to know. Is that what you want to hear?"

"Good man." Samuel Ramsay flips him a card with a telephone number written across it. "Nice to catch up with you again."

Mocet watches the bounty hunter leave. It's only as Ramsay reaches the door that Stephan asks if he's forgetting something. "What is this? Take your box with you!"

Cursing to himself, Samuel Ramsay retraces his steps. "I almost forgot. Damn jet lag playing tricks on my memory." He peels open the flaps, smiling as he catches Mocet's eye, and then reaches inside with both hands. "I brought a gift for you."

The bullion launderer takes a moment to register that the object placed under the light from the lamp, with hair matted thickly, is the severed head of a bull terrier. It rests at an awkward angle. Both eyes are rolled back. The tongue, hanging slack, is much darker than it should be. One more awful second passes before he recognizes the blood-soaked offering.

"My dog!" he whispers in horror, and drags his eyes back to the man behind this atrocity. "You've been to my house?"

"Why did you lie to me, Stephan? I asked you a straight and simple question. You couldn't look me in the eye when you answered, which tells me you're keeping the truth from me. Now I'm going to ask you one more time. Has Beth Nelson been here? If I don't hear what I need to know, then you can expect your daughter's pretty head to arrive before close of business. *Do I make myself clear?*"

Samuel Ramsay delivers this final threat with sudden fury in his voice. The man who has just found himself face-to-face with the slain family pet pulls back in his seat. He shows his palms, pale and sweating now.

"She called me. From a pay phone. The exchange is all set up."

With a smile of satisfaction, the bounty hunter nods to himself.

"Thank you, Stephan. That wasn't so difficult, was it?"

WHEN WILSON ARRIVES FOR THE NEXT SHIFT, HE FINDS ME AT THE screens in the monitoring room.

"For a kid on a mission, you look like you've suffered a setback." Dropping his newspaper on the desk, he takes the seat beside me. "Has Cleopatra let you down?"

For a moment I wonder if I shouldn't just open up to Wilson one more time. I've had a whole day to dwell on the fact that when I next go home, Beth will not be there. Then I tell myself to focus on the task ahead. I'm gutted about her decision, but there's work to be done, and not just for my sake but also for her. She may have decided to move on without me, but in many ways we will always be united in our desire to stay free. So I turn to face Wilson and gesture at the screens.

"I'll find out what's on Cleo's mind just as soon as Mr. Thorn leaves the building," I tell him.

On the monitor, the security director can be seen walking

across the lobby with Sara Sinclair. Both have finished work for the day, but I can't truly begin until they're gone.

Wilson watches them enter the security pod, one after the other. On my journey here the rain was beginning to come down hard. Unlike me, both Sinclair and Thorn are carrying umbrellas. "The next time I head out that way," he tells me, "I won't be coming back."

I look across at him. "It's your last shift tonight?" I had completely forgotten. I've become so consumed by Cleo and now Beth that his departure has just slipped from my mind. "Did Thorn give you a going-away present or anything?"

"A pat on the back and a positive reference."

"Is that all?"

"I'm not complaining," he assures me. "The new job sounds like it'll suit me just fine. Plenty of time for writing. The big difference is that I won't have a computer breathing down my neck."

I glance back at the monitors. It confirms that we are in sole charge once more.

"I'm in two minds about computers," I say, reaching for the keyboard so I can log in. "They've opened up a lot of possibilities— and brought me more trouble than I could ever imagine."

Wilson nods, considering what I have said. Rising from the seat, I let him know that he can find me in the control hub.

"Hey, you go ahead and take care of your future," he tells me, and peels open his newspaper. "So long as I can look forward to a quiet last night, then I'm happy."

Dropping into the seat in front of the great pyramid, I still feel strangely uncomfortable once again. Maybe it's her sheer size, or the fact that I have barely scratched the surface when it comes to understanding her. Either way, I don't like feeling this rattled. All I can think is that progress will ease my anxieties.

"It's going to be a long night," I say out loud, drumming my fingers on the surface of the desk. "By the end of it, I hope you're going to be my eyes and ears inside the computer networks of the CIA and the American military. Just don't freak out on me," I add quickly. "I know how to get inside. I just need you to be cool and keep me posted on their efforts to catch up with yours truly."

I fall quiet there, watching her lights blink for a moment, and then reach for the telephone.

The weakest link in any secure system is always human. Willard Thorn demonstrated this by relying on his judgment when it came to hiring me. The same could be said for America's most guarded computer networks. I have accessed her military system many times. It's just a question of calling one of the service department administrators, such as catering or cleaning, and I've committed several numbers to memory.

First I dial into a private exchange owned by a group of Swiss hackers. I place the call through the speakers as it begins to ring. After ten seconds, a short silence precedes another dial tone. This one I know leaves me untraceable. Before I make the call, I summon a Web browser and access my online e-mail account. I have never used it for correspondence, of course, but the storage space is useful for software. Here I keep a neat little antitracking program. Once I fire it up, I'm free to visit websites knowing that I've been shuttled randomly through hundreds of servers to get there.

"Let's call sanitation," I say. "They're always harassed in that department."

I punch in the number. As the line clicks over and then begins to ring, I direct the browser to a classified military server. Of course, this gets me to a page requesting both my user name and password. It also carries a simple warning against unauthorized access. Should anyone attempt to gain entrance without authorization, the virtual dogs would be unleashed. I've no intention of taking such a risk. In order to get inside, I simply have to persuade an employee to part with the required information.

"Sanitation. United States Southern Command. Glover speaking."

The voice on the other end of the line is male, Midwest, and midthirties. It also sounds a little like the guy just woke up.

"Staff Sergeant?" I say, in a Yankee accent that Beth helped me to refine. "Staff Sergeant Glover?"

"Private Glover," the voice replies, sharpening up some now. "Who is this?"

Now that I know his name and rank, I draw breath to assert my authority and annoyance at his very existence.

"You're talking to *Warrant Officer* DiMatteo from Inter-departmental System Securities. Private, do you realize how close you are to a court-martial for dereliction of duty?"

"*Sir?*"

I smile to myself. This guy is on the back foot already. So long as I keep talking at him, sounding like I'm in a hurry, I feel sure he'll crumble.

"Our servers are under siege twenty-four hours a day from professional hackers and wannabe punks. These worms would sell their mothers for a way in, but that can't happen so long as we follow procedures. Simple things like ensuring your password isn't so easy a child could crack it. Now, I'm looking at a list of all passwords in use across the service departments down there, and yours is flashing up for being as dumb as they come."

Silence. I can almost hear him swallowing.

"With respect," he reasons, "we change the passwords every week here."

"Let me guess," I reply. "You're tired of coming up with a new one every seven days, right?"

Another pause. "It isn't easy, sir, but I hear what you're saying."

Of course, I have no idea what password this guy is using. All I can be certain about is that when faced with renewing it on a regular basis, most people default to tacking on a number to the word they've memorized and simply adding to it each time. Had my friend here not sounded so shamefaced and foolish, I would've simply asked him to stay alert and closed the call. It may not have gotten me anywhere, but I would've done the military a small favor. Instead I sense poor Private Glover has been caught out by my bluff, so I tell him I shall stay on the line while he makes the necessary change.

"I don't want to know the new password, Private. I just want to be assured that you're using a combination of case-sensitive letters and numbers."

"I'll reset it immediately, sir. . . . Okay, it's asking me for a new password."

"I see that," I lie. "And if you'll just confirm your user name."

There comes a time in a conversation like this where it's possible to come out of nowhere with a question and get what you want. Much like a sucker punch in the boxing ring, it's a matter of quickly wearing down your opponent, just as I've done, and identifying when his guard drops.

"Uh, that'll be Jake-dot-Glover. Should the password have a certain number of characters?"

"Eight, minimum," I say, my fingers darting across the keyboard. With the user name field complete, and knowing he has yet to submit the new password he's concocting, I hit the enter key. A new page builds on my screen. I am inside the system, a moment I mark by sighing and tutting to myself. "Private, we have a minor glitch with the password protocol. You can try to reset it, but I suspect it won't recognize that you've logged out. Can you try for me?"

"Sure thing." I hear him striking the keys. "You're right. It's saying I'm still logged in."

"Damn it. I'll need to reboot the program. Give me a moment, okay?"

"Go for it. I'll grab a coffee."

"Don't leave your station," I order him, as I upload the program that will record every keystroke he goes on to make. Naturally, I'd love to have the time it afforded, but no internal security adviser would allow for that. "Okay," I say, on logging out. "Try it now."

I sit back as the speakers play out his attempt. He coughs and plugs away at his keyboard, before confirming that all is well.

"Keep it that way," I say, before wishing him a good day. Having cut the call, I open up the key-logging software and summon a report from Glover's workstation. The list that scrolls down is a live record. It's growing very slowly, a measure of the private's poor typing ability, but provides his new password: 1nv1nc1BLe.

Chuckling to myself, I call up Cleopatra's user interface.

"Are you ready for a new challenge?" I ask. "Then we shall begin."

29

INTO THE EARLY HOURS, I WORK HARD AT CREATING NEW COMMANDS.
I use Cleo's basic ability to assess an environment and then tailor
it to meet my needs. As I get to grips with her capacity to make
some decisions for herself, I find it helps me avoid brooding
about Beth. By the time I'm ready to send her into the military
system, I just have to check the key-logging software to confirm
that Private Glover has signed off for the day. With my heart
quickening, I provide Cleo with the password I captured from
him. At the same time, I hear a sound. It makes me jump. I look
up to see Wilson at the balcony door.

"Up to no good?" he asks.

I draw breath to spin him a story and then think better of
it. I have already opened up to Wilson about why I am here. It
doesn't seem necessary to lie to him now.

"I'm just trying to do the right thing for myself," I tell him.
"I'm not a bad person, but if I'm ever captured they'll treat me

like a terror suspect. I'll have no opportunity to defend myself. No hope of clearing my name."

Wilson hears me out, and then nods to himself like he has no argument.

"I've checked out the main floor," he says next. "One thing I won't miss is that nightly tour of duty."

"To be honest," I tell him, "that element of the job creeps me out."

"Sphinx is a big place, but you'll get used to it." With a glance at the giant mainframe, Wilson steps inside. "So what progress have you made?"

"You really want to know?" I ask, half smiling now.

"It's a second education, my friend. From the army onward, I've always been a slave to the system. I never dreamed it could be beaten."

As Wilson comes around to look at the screen, I tell him at this moment Cleopatra is inside a server belonging to the U.S. military. I explain that I've instructed her to mine the entire system for information about me. There's no need to search for intelligence on Beth, I add, because on paper she's dead.

"All this is possible from here?" Wilson steps around the desk to watch me at work.

"I can't say for sure," I say with a shrug. "I'm working on the basis that closed computer systems usually devote their efforts to securing the perimeter. The administrators take the view that the World Wide Web is hostile territory. Certainly the military deploy firewalls with every defense feature going."

"Like a fort?"

"That's about right," I say. "But once you've worked out how to gain access, generally less attention is paid to the security between departments and even associate networks like the CIA. It doesn't matter if you have to virtually surface through the toilet bowl to get inside, you'd be surprised how easy it is to work your way to the top. Now that we're in, she's on her way. I've shown Cleopatra how to look for vulnerabilities in the system she can exploit. It isn't just blank passwords that she's looking for. She might find that the user name I hijacked has privileges she can use to gain access to an account belonging to someone more senior, and so on. It's a question of digital leapfrog, while picking up intelligence and covering your tracks along the way."

Wilson studies the monitors. I return my attention to the code on the left-hand screen and begin to rewrite a line. A moment later I hear him curse under his breath. I find his gaze locked on the other screen. It's still on default, showing a top-down, wireframe view of the building. Sure enough, two green lights indicate our presence in the control hub.

What has caused his eyes to pinch at the corners is the red light blinking outside the perimeter.

"Who can that be?" asks Wilson. "At this hour?"

There are two lights, I realize then, floating very close to each other just beyond the main door.

"Let's see." From the command list I request the security camera directory. Cleopatra responds by clearing the code from the left-hand monitor. In its place, we find ourselves viewing a grid of closed-circuit cameras. It's the same layout as in the monitoring room, except every feed is much smaller.

Despite the scale, the image from the external camera over the main door is clear enough. I don't recognize the figure with the blowtorch, defiant in the downpour. Only the female under his control. One I did not expect to see for some time, and certainly not under such circumstances. He yanks her head back by the hair, forcing her to cower from the ice-blue jet of flame.

"Beth!"

30

IN SHOCK AND PANIC, I RISE FROM THE SEAT AND JUST STARE AT THE
screen. I am dumbstruck. A string of questions race through my
mind, only one of which I can answer.

"That's your girl?" Wilson sounds as rattled as I feel. "Who
is that guy?"

"I've never laid eyes on him before," I say, "but I know full
well what he wants."

After a moment, Wilson's eyes widen. "My God, he's come
for you!"

On the screen, I watch the figure with the blowtorch shout
something at the camera. He's in his late forties, bulked out, and
bearded, but carries the kind of purpose and weight in his eyes
that tells me he could inflict violence at any time. Beth looks
absolutely terrified. She's drenched and sobbing. I look at her
in his clutches and my stomach twists. I don't know how this
individual has tracked us down, but I feel sure that gold bar she

intended to cash must be involved. Whatever the case, right now I feel her life is in my hands.

"What's he saying?" I ask, as the man appears to yell into the lens once more.

"Every camera is wired for sound," Wilson tells me. He leans across to the monitor, jabs at the feed in question, and drags it diagonally with his fingertip. Immediately it expands to fill the monitor, bringing with it an overlay of control icons. "I've seen the tech guys do that," he adds.

I had no idea the screen is touch sensitive. Missing such a simple trick just serves to remind me that I am really not in control here at all. Scrambling into action now, I slide up the volume bar and drop back into the seat as a voice consumes the room.

"... *immediately, Carl. Get yourself out here right away, or the girl dies for real this time!*"

Without thinking, I stab at the microphone icon. "I hear you!" I yell. "I'm listening, okay? Just calm down! Ease up, please!"

I know the external speaker is working, because the man tips his head up as I address him.

"*There you are!*" he calls back in a gruff American accent. "*Do I need to repeat my request?*"

"Don't hurt her!" I plead. "I'll do whatever you want, but leave Beth out of this."

"Come outside, Carl. I am not playing a game here. Is that quite clear?" the man shouts to be heard over the downpour. I see no sign that he's enjoying this moment of control, however. He certainly isn't toying with me in any way, just as he's stated. *"Make one wrong move and I'll start out by blinding her, one eye at a time, do you understand me? My brief is to bring you in unharmed, but if I have to kill to catch up with you, then I will not hesitate. Collateral damage is not a problem for me. Not a problem at all. Come quietly, Carl, and I'll spare her sight. Hey, I'll even let her go! How about that?"*

If his manner is direct, his appearance is disarming. Everything from the beard to the anorak and crumpled slacks makes him look more like a man worn down at the edges. Without the cruel advantage he has here, he'd look all washed up. As it is, I know I'm looking at an individual who clearly has some history and experience in this line of work.

"There's no way he can break in from the outside." This is Wilson, drawing my attention once more. I find him staring at the mainframe, as if he's addressing Cleopatra herself. "This place is indestructible."

"We're not done yet." I punch open the microphone to address the man outside. My heart is screaming at me to agree to his demand. It's my head that tells me I should bid to buy some time. "I can open up," I tell him. "I just need to figure out how to override the locks. Everything is computer controlled."

"Then you're the right guy for the job," replies the bearded man. *"Open the door, Hobbes."*

"Give me the time and I can do it."

All of a sudden he looks mightily annoyed. For a moment I think he is going to prove what he can do. Instead, to my great relief, he shoots his cuff and reads his wristwatch.

"You have less than thirty minutes, Carl. Beth will suffer unless you present yourself to me in that time!"

31

WHAT DO I KNOW ABOUT THIS GUY? FOR ONE, HIS SHAMBLING appearance masks an individual of some confidence, ingenuity, and purpose. That he's brandishing a blowtorch as a weapon suggests a taste for torture or some creativity in his methods. I'm praying it's the latter. I just hope I'm not right on both counts. At the same time his promise not to harm her so long as I follow instructions seems genuine. It makes me think he's in control of his actions. Someone ruthless but not insane. That has to be marginally better than facing a psychopath who might snake on the deal for the thrill of the kill.

Then again, I truly believe he will not hesitate to turn that flame on Beth unless I hand myself over to him.

For a moment after closing communications, I stare at the screen and struggle to think. I can hear Wilson tell me we should just call the police, but he isn't really looking at the bigger picture. Naturally I am prepared to do anything to save Beth at this time. Even if it means losing our liberty, I would summon the law. However, I just know that she would be maimed or dead at the first wail of a siren.

"I need to find out more about this guy," I say, mostly to myself. "I have to work out who I'm up against."

"Isn't that evident?"

If Wilson had begun to recover his composure, he seems understandably rattled once again. I stare at the screen, contemplating my next move, only to find my attention drawn by a grid of lights blinking rapidly within the mainframe. I figure it's indicating some kind of data process, which is when I recall that Cleopatra is currently undertaking a task for me. Immediately I collapse the bank of camera feeds. Underneath, I find her running a file scan on the military server. Already she is 92 percent through it. As a result, she has almost completed a list of files that mention my name.

"Okay," I say, thinking ahead now. "Let's find out if the guy is here on official business."

"You can do that?" Wilson comes around the desk as I begin to work through the files. Mostly it's e-mail correspondence going way back through the years. At a glance, it all appears to be associated with my disappearance, and I know all about that. With the scan complete, I swiftly arrange everything in date order. Now things look more promising. For near the top of the list is a document entitled "Fugitive Status." This one, I note, is a shared document between the military and the CIA.

"You're on the money." Wilson is practically breathing down my neck now.

"Here we go," I say, and open it up.

We are presented with a series of head shots. Twenty in total. Some are official military identification photos. Others are less detailed and taken at long range. They represent different nationalities, and there are several women, too. All feature names and numbers underneath.

"America's Most Wanted," says Wilson. "So what does this tell us?"

"That our man isn't on the list," I suggest. "Unlike me."

Sure enough, my face is featured in the selection. A picture taken on my arrival at Camp Twilight. So much has happened since then that I barely recognize myself. I feel like I've aged beyond my years, though in the picture I'm still the youngest of them all by a long way. I'm also the only one to feature a band across the picture marked CLASSIFIED.

"Son, you're a state secret."

"Seems that way." I draw the cursor over my picture. With a click, I am taken to a page providing intelligence reports in the hunt for me. I am wise to many of them, seeing that I set up supposed sightings to keep the authorities busy. What interests me is the latest report. I open it up. Within the top-line bullet points, I find myself looking at a number in bold with a lot of zeros attached to it.

"Look at that!" Wilson whistles and takes to the seat beside me. "You're worth a lot of dough to them. If I wasn't such a nice guy, I'd turn you in myself!"

I sit back in my chair and face him side on. "It means our friend outside is a bounty hunter."

Wilson nods, still reading the screen. "The good news is they want you alive."

"Under the circumstances, that doesn't make me feel much better." I scroll down through the report. It mentions no names. Nor does it give any indication of progress made following some high-level meeting in which the price on my head was addressed. I reach the end, none the wiser.

Dwelling on the man's identity, I switch back to the exterior camera feed. Beth and the bounty hunter are only just in the frame. The rain is hammering down, but I know he's not here seeking shelter.

"Maybe you should communicate," suggests Wilson. "For her sake, let him know you're working on the door."

I think about it for a beat, considering what I might gain. "You know what?" I say eventually. "There might well be something in bringing him into shot once more." I reach across to touch the microphone icon. "We're making progress," I report. "I'm doing everything I can to open up the door without triggering the alarm system."

On the screen, the bounty hunter looks up and then drags Beth back out into the rain. He reminds me of the time I have left, but I'm not listening. Instead I hover my finger over the pause icon and stab at it as soon as he looks directly into the lens. At once the image freezes.

"Okay," says Wilson, clearly several steps behind me. "What now?"

"We ask Cleopatra to run a visual search inside the network for any image that resembles this one." I type as I talk, copying the code that drives her facial recognition system and adding it to a new line of instruction. "If this guy knows about the bounty," I say, on running the search, "then surely the authorities must know about *him*."

The cursor turns for what seems like an age. Once again, I feel as if I'm communicating with someone of huge intelligence using only a very basic understanding of their language. If this was some kind of alien encounter, I think to myself all of a sudden, chances are I would be crushed. I am about to abandon the plan when a picture pops up, followed by several others.

"Cleo's missed the mark," observes Wilson, and he's right. Two of the head shots are clearly military personnel, while the other looks way too young. What they have in common, I realize, is a trim beard and some likeness in the shape of their eyes and noses.

When the final image appears, sharing much the same look but for the thicker facial hair, it is clear to us both that we have our man.

"Samuel Ramsay," I declare, on opening the file in which the image is embedded. I fall quiet for a moment, reading the history of this rogue CIA agent, and sense my heart sinking. "This isn't good," I say to Wilson finally. That he fails to reply tells me he has reached the same view. "This isn't good at all."

32

A WOLF IS AT OUR DOOR. IN THE YEARS SINCE THE MAN OUTSIDE SOLD out on the CIA, he appears to have forged a reputation as a hunter. One who tracks down people for a bounty, no matter where they are in the world, and brings them in dead or alive. Just glancing at the reports of the brutal range of methods he employs, I can't help thinking that those he has been contracted to kill outright were spared a great deal of suffering. Judging by his form, it is clear that if I put up a fight he will punish me for it before delivering me to his paymasters.

"This guy," says Wilson, reading the screen alongside me, "just whose side is he on?"

I understand why he has raised the question. According to the details, the majority of individuals Ramsay has captured were not all wanted by the Americans, or any other Western government. Terror organizations have also sought the services of Samuel Ramsay, who has carried out everything from kidnapping to assassination by order.

"It seems he takes commission from all sides," I say. "That sounds to me like a man who will do whatever it takes so long as he's paid in full."

"With that figure on your head," says Wilson, "what are the chances that he'll grow tired and just go away?"

I don't answer. I say nothing because my only option, it seems, is to give myself up. Now that I know the man's name and reputation, I cannot afford to let Beth suffer in any way. I might not have liked her decision to move on, but that didn't stop me caring for her any less.

"I'm going out there," I tell Wilson, and rise from my seat. "What else can I do?"

Wilson looks taken aback. He watches me head around for the balcony door.

"You're giving up the fight? Just like that?"

I turn to face him. "Let Mr. Thorn know I changed my mind about the job. What I've done here might even make him realize that there's no such thing as a secure system. Who knows? He might even consider keeping you on."

"Wait a minute!" Wilson is on his feet, some steel in his voice now. "When you came clean about your real identity and I finally believed you, it totally blew me away. You also impressed the hell out of me. Sphinx might not be as watertight as Thorn likes to think, but I don't know anyone else who could've punctured through as you have. You got American intelligence hunting high and low for you, and yet here you are recruiting the help of a supercomputer to keep them at bay. Carl, you're running rings around them!"

"Until today," I point out, which stalls him for a moment. "Right now I just feel trapped."

"You're not beat, son. Not yet. This is a one-man war you're fighting, and I'm speaking as an old soldier. Okay, so you've been ambushed, but you can't admit defeat until every option has been explored and exhausted."

"What options?" I ask. "Minutes from now, Beth is going to get hurt unless I leave this building!"

"A storm is coming down out there," he says with a shrug and a hint of a grin. "Why don't you invite them inside?"

33

BEFORE ADDRESSING THE BOUNTY HUNTER OVER THE MICROPHONE, I ask Wilson for a moment of silence.

"I need to clear my head," I tell him. "Because right now my voice of reason is yelling at me not to do this."

"It's crazy," he agrees, "but if you can draw him through the doors, it gives you a fighting chance."

Wilson doesn't need to explain his reasons any further. Even though I have a long way to go before Cleopatra comes under my complete control, I do at least know how Sphinx Cargo operates. I understand the system, as any hacker should before striking. If I can bring Samuel Ramsay within these walls, then at the very least I'll be facing him within an environment I know inside out. Still shaken by what's happened, I draw down the command menu and begin to work through it.

"Thorn told me that ultimately Cleopatra dictates who passes through the doors," I say, but not as a warning, because at the same time I find what I'm looking for. I turn to face Wilson and grin. "I guess he didn't realize he was talking to someone who'd consider that to be a challenge."

For a building boasting such high-end security measures, I discover I can disable every sensor and alarm at a keystroke. This doesn't come as much of a surprise, however. In designing the setup here, all the efforts went into protecting access to Cleopatra rather than safeguarding her capabilities. Much as it pains me, it also means I can switch off the aggressive measures the bounty hunter would face as soon as he stepped inside. As Beth has no such authorization either, it's the only way I can prevent her from being taken out as well.

Now, swallowing uncomfortably because my mouth is bone-dry, I summon the external camera feed and bring the microphone online. The speakers click with static, which must be relayed outside, for Samuel Ramsay steps into the frame. He drags Beth with him; she cowers from the blowtorch as he blasts it into life.

"Where are you, Carl? Time's up."

I hold the microphone open but say nothing. Wilson looks at me with dread in his expression. He gestures at the screen, urging me to say something.

"I can compromise the software that controls the lock," I announce finally. "But the door is going to open for only a minute. After that, an emergency system kicks in to close it again."

"So do it!" spits Ramsay, strengthening his hold on Beth.

"Listen," I say pleadingly. "Once I type in the command, it's going to take me more than sixty seconds to reach the main doors from where I am now. I'll never make it out in time!"

"Don't make me blind the girl, Hobbes!"

"It's all I can do," I reply, and kill the communication.

I find Wilson simply staring at me. "This is how you operate?" he asks. "Man, that takes some guts."

I should tell him this is the biggest gamble I have ever taken in my life. The sixty-second window I plucked out of thin air. On disabling the main door locking mechanism, it would remain that way unless I chose to reset it again. I sold the line to Ramsay simply to increase the pressure on him to come to me. Online and over the phone, I've often called on the power of persuasion to encourage key operatives to unwittingly help me gain access to computer networks. Mostly it involves pushing them just to the limit of their patience so they give me what I want. I cut off the conversation with Ramsay at a critical time. He heard me out and then made a threat to harm Beth in the worst way if I didn't comply.

Now all I can do is hope that my silence fires him up to come to me. The alternative is just unthinkable.

177

Immediately I turn my attention to the overhead layout on the second monitor. Beth and the bounty hunter are still represented by red lights. I touch the main door. On the screen, I am invited to choose between a status check and an override. I choose the latter and watch the door swing outward.

On the camera feed, Samuel Ramsay can be seen switching his attention to the door, which has just cracked ajar.

"Go on," I mutter to myself, aware that Beth could suffer very badly if I have misjudged this man. "Take the damn bait."

34

WITH A SENSE OF RELIEF AND RISING DREAD, I WATCH THE TWO RED lights drift across the atrium layout.

"Whatever you want me to do," says Wilson, "just say the word."

I draw down Cleopatra's command menu, working as quickly as I can.

"I need you to stay right here," I say. "Ramsay thinks I'm alone, and it's in our interest to keep it like that. While I'm away, you're in control of the air-conditioning."

"Huh?"

In response, I select an atrium camera. On the screen, Ramsay can be seen clutching Beth by her upper arm. He's looking around; waiting for me, it seems.

"I'm on my way," I announce over the speaker. "See that door at the top of the open stairs? You'll find me on the other side."

"I want you out here, Hobbes. What part of that don't you understand?"

"If you want to leave with me," I tell the bounty hunter, "I'll need to show Beth how to override the locks. That can only be done from the back end of the building, which is where I am as I speak to you."

I see Ramsay draw breath to bark some response and let him hear the click of the microphone shutting down once more.

"In his shoes," says Wilson, "I'd be furious with you."

"Good," I reply. "Because when you're angry, you don't think straight—and that's all I can ask of him right now."

"So what do you want me to do?" he asks, nodding at Cleopatra. "You've already turned up the heat, Carl. I'm not sure I can make it any hotter."

I click on a command option. The screen switches to a bank of dials. A fader sits beneath it, which I draw across with the mouse. "It isn't the air temperature that could help us here," I say, as several dial needles begin to rise. "It's the oxygen." I give Wilson a moment to realize that I have just opened up the nitrogen supply to the cargo hold.

"I see where you're going with this," says Wilson, as the needles fall still. I've just left the cargo floor with only 10 percent of oxygen in the air. With the nitrogen level at 90 percent, this is way over the danger threshold Thorn mentioned to me.

"I just wish I could be sure you'll make it back."

"That makes two of us," I tell him, before hurrying across to the balcony door.

Wilson takes my place behind the monitors and tells me to be lucky.

"Just be sure to bring Beth back in one piece," he adds. "I'd like to meet the young lady."

I press my lips together, suddenly reminded of what has happened between us.

"Last night," I tell him, "Beth and I went our separate ways."

Wilson looks baffled, but only for a moment. "That isn't how it looks from here," he replies. "Go get your girl, Carl."

Inside the airlock, I snap on the breathing apparatus. Next I collect the second mask and tank at my feet and tell myself to stay calm. This isn't easy. From the moment Samuel Ramsay appeared in the picture, I feel as if I have been moving in fast-forward. For a moment I listen to myself inhaling and exhaling through the mask. Then, with a hiss, the door slides open onto the walkway.

I swallow uncomfortably and step out onto the gantry. At the far end, beyond the airlock, I know the bounty hunter will be waiting for me. I move swiftly under the low lights, though I feel like a dead man walking. Throughout, I keep Beth in mind.

I am terrified of what I am about to face, but I break into a sprint for her sake.

At the far end, I slam my palm against the intercom.

"I'm here," I report, and release the button for a beat so he cannot hear me breathing through the mask. "Just promise me you won't harm Beth. For one thing, you need her in a fit state to override the lock to the main door. We're all sealed in now. She's your only chance of getting out."

"So show her what she has to do and let's get going. C'mon, Hobbes!"

I switch my attention to the airlock control. From here, I can operate both entry and exit points. I open up the atrium side and then invite the bounty hunter to step right in.

"All it'll do is dust you down," I assure him. "You can relax."

As I speak, I have to remind myself that Samuel Ramsay will be unaware that he's just walked into an airlock. There is no warning sign on that side, and the breathing apparatus is stored away and out of sight. I just hope I've gained his trust enough for him not to question me. When I hear movement from the other side, I know he is almost where I want him.

"I'll blind her, Hobbes," he calls through, at which I hear Beth gasp. *"If you're fooling with me, she loses an eye."*

I have no doubt that Ramsay has just positioned the blow-torch in order to carry out his threat. I just hope that I am right about what will happen a moment from now.

I brace myself for the door to slide open. As it does so, a hiss kicks in like the sound of a tire deflating. Knowing that the nitrogen gas has just forced the breathable air from the pod, I come face-to-face with the bounty hunter. The look of surprise on his face isn't just down to his blowtorch suddenly going out. In an environment I have virtually stripped of oxygen, it's his lungs that fail to work as well.

"Don't inhale!" I yell at Beth, reaching in to grab her. "It could kill you!"

Samuel Ramsay responds by lashing out at me with one fist. I twist away, but in doing so drop the second tank and mask. In desperation, I try to scoop it up. Ramsay sees me go down, however. He kicks it from my reach and then brings his knee into my chest. I reel backward, dragging Beth down with me, and see the tank roll under the walkway railings. Desperately I try to grab the tube with the mask attached. My fingers touch the strap, only for it all to snake right over the edge.

Ramsay is bearing over me now with a wild look in his eyes. I plant my foot in his stomach, kicking hard. He doubles up some, losing his grip on Beth as well as what little air is left in his lungs. Seizing the moment, I rise up and shove him hard in the chest with both hands. Off balance, and with both arms flailing, Ramsay crashes back into the airlock. Without hesitation I hit the console switch. He sees the door sliding across to seal him in and lunges for me. I am too slow to stop the bounty hunter from grabbing my shirt at the collar, but there is nothing he can do to prevent the door from trapping his forearm.

"Give it up!" I yell through my face mask. "Let it shut or you'll die!"

Through the gap, I find myself eye-to-eye with the man. He's glaring at me, puce with rage and desperate to breathe in. "I'll see you on the flip side," he snarls, making one vain attempt to rip off my mask before snatching his arm back through the gap.

"Carl, help me!"

The voice brings me wheeling around. Beth is struggling to stand. She has one hand at her throat, fighting the instinct to inhale. Taking a deep breath, I snap off my mask and plug it around her mouth. Beth gulps down the air, her shoulders rising and falling. Indicating that we need to move fast, I pull her up onto her feet.

Sure enough, judging by the muffled sound of a locker slamming, it seems the bounty hunter has found himself some breathing apparatus. With my arms around Beth, I hurry her back across the walkway. Every step I take is an effort, but I can't afford to stop and take a hit from the mask.

Not when the airlock opens behind us once more.

I reel around, but see no sign of the bounty hunter. Just an empty chamber. Then I hear a noise from below. The sound, perhaps, of someone dropping from the walkway.

"I convinced him you'd be armed," says Beth, sounding muffled through the mask. "I wanted to give you a chance!"

In trouble now, with my heart, head, and lungs feeling close to exploding, I double my efforts to reach the other side. If Samuel Ramsay is hoping to ambush us, I fear he may pounce as I seek to access the other airlock.

On seeing the door open up as we approach, however, I know that someone is watching over us.

I throw myself in with Beth, spinning out now. As the door closes, Beth presses the mask to my face. She holds it there as I breathe and then grins with me as the airlock draws out the gas and fills it with oxygen.

When the gallery side opens up, we find Wilson waiting anxiously.

"This is Beth," I croak, as he helps us to exit the pod.

"Carl spoke highly of you," she tells him. "I can see why."

Beth's voice is still as shot as mine, but I'm elated by the fact that her spirit is intact. Wilson, meanwhile, looks as pale as she does.

"It's far from over," he says, addressing me now. He gestures toward the control hub. "Carl, the wireframe is showing another red light in the building."

35

SABINE-I-SABAH SLIPPED INTO THE UNITED KINGDOM ON JUST ONE
previous occasion. Back then, during the latter years of Saddam's
reign, her mission was to seduce an exiled Iraqi television
journalist. One who had just begun investigating corruption
within the regime. It took only a month for him to fall deeply in
love and confide in her about the high-risk documentary he was
making. Another week passed before he named his informants
within the Iraqi ruling party. In response, Sabine had kissed him
on the lips, then shot him through the heart.

This time, working for a different paymaster, the assassin
would make no such charm offensive before moving in for the
kill. According to Sabine's Al-Qaeda contact, this was about retribution. *Make Carl Hobbes pay,* she has been instructed. *Show
him no mercy or dignity in death. Photograph the evidence.*

As soon as her contact revealed that the CIA was offering a
rich reward to bring him in alive, Sabine knew who would be on

his trail. Shadowing Samuel Ramsay had taught her many things about the man. He was ruthless and efficient, at odds with his disorderly appearance, and would clearly stop at nothing in his bid to reach the boy.

A surprise, then, that the bounty hunter has just made an almighty mess of claiming his prize. Sabine had observed the whole incident from the shadows. Having first slipped through the security pod behind Ramsay and the girl who served as his bargaining chip, she had watched him walk into some kind of trap. Whatever ambush occurred on the other side of that door at the top of the steps had both surprised and enraged the man. Only when he reappeared and found himself a breathing tank did it become clear to her that somehow in there Hobbes had control of the oxygen levels.

Now, collecting the last tank for herself, the assassin tests the door to the airlock. It slides open without resistance. Noting the retinal scanner, she concludes that Hobbes must have disengaged it from the inside to draw Ramsay through. She steps into the pod, strapping on her mask at the same time, and braces herself to take control of the situation.

When the door slides open onto the walkway, Sabine-i-Sabah emerges with a pistol drawn in both hands. She's wearing a dark tunic shirt over trousers, and her long hair is tied back by a silk band. It's an elegant yet practical look. One that also hides a military web belt containing everything she needs to see this job through.

Dropping to one knee now, she scans the space around her. It's an impressive environment, but now is not the time to take in the artifacts and bullion bars in storage here. Sabine creeps forward, moving fluidly, only to freeze at a sound from below. With her finger tight around the trigger, she creeps to the edge and looks over the rail.

Through the gloom, directly underneath her, the assassin lays eyes on the man she has followed across continents. Samuel Ramsay may have an oxygen supply as she does, but this environment is about to prove deadly for an entirely different reason.

36

I STARE AT THE SCREEN IN STUNNED SILENCE. SO TOO DO WILSON AND Beth. Seeing yet another red light within the wireframe leaves me feeling like a trapped animal.

"Judging by their movement," suggests Wilson, "I'd say our friend on the floor is unaware that he has company."

I glance at Beth. She looks as shaken as I feel. "Samuel Ramsay is the name of your buddy out there," I say. "We're dealing with a bounty hunter who has no intention of snatching anything from this building but me."

Beth turns to me now. Before she draws breath to speak, I can see something weighing heavily on her mind. "Carl, I—"

"It's done now," I say to reassure her. "That gold bar you'd stashed away was bound to bring us trouble. You cashed it in, right? Broke your cover and got this in return?"

Beth looks to the floor. At the same time, one of the red lights begins to move through the wireframe. In silence, we watch it gravitate between the pallet stacks on the cargo floor. The second light, up there on the walkway, remains quite still. I realize that this blocks any chance we have of escaping. Without taking my eyes off the screen, I summon the cameras for a closer look.

"Oh, man," says Wilson as I select a feed from over the walkway. "Is this good news or bad?"

It takes a moment for me to realize that the crouching figure up there is female. She's brandishing a handgun, and when she reaches to adjust some kind of holster under her tunic, I see several blades as well. What's most striking about her, however, is that she looks weirdly familiar.

"Something tells me this is no thief," remarks Beth. "It takes one to know one, after all."

"If she's known to the authorities," I suggest, jabbing at the keyboard as I speak, "we can identify her." Having programmed the supercomputer to seek out a visual match for Samuel Ramsay, I find I can cook up a second request in no time. "Cleo is a fast learner," I add, on feeding her a freeze-frame of the figure out there. "She knows what to do now."

"I wish we could say the same for ourselves," murmurs Beth.

From the cargo floor, Samuel Ramsay can be heard bellowing my name.

"I'm not here to hurt you, Hobbes. Let me make that quite clear.

But if you want to fool with me, I won't hesitate to kill Beth! I'll come for her first, man, unless you give yourself up to me right now!"

I realize we have little time left before he finds the airlock down below. At any moment we could hear him thunder up the spiral staircase and lay waste to any options we might have left.

"Those oxygen tanks will last thirty minutes max," observes Wilson. "Somehow I don't think Ramsay will need one for that long."

"Can we seal off the airlocks?" asks Beth. "If we can trap them out there, it'll give us a chance to negotiate at least."

Wilson shakes his head. "They can always be opened from the inside," he says. "In an oxygen-depleted environment, it's a necessary safety precaution."

"And a security flaw," I mutter, struggling to think how we might turn this to our advantage.

For a moment there is silence. I feel almost resigned, wondering if I should just surrender for the sake of Wilson and Beth. Then Cleopatra returns with the results of her search of the military servers. This time, she brings only one return. Immediately I realize why I feel like I've seen her before. For the image has been plucked from the "Fugitive Status" file. A dossier of America's Most Wanted that also included me.

It takes just a click to put a name to the face of the woman on the walkway.

"Sabine-i-Sabah," I say, scanning her intelligence report. I only need to read a few lines to realize what we're facing here. While the authorities placed a ransom on my head, I learn that the assassin out there is under precise orders from Al-Qaeda to sever it completely. "Okay, so she isn't someone who can help us," I add, and quickly rise to my feet. "We really need to leave this building."

Wilson continues gazing at the screen. "Even if she chooses to follow Ramsay to the floor, crossing the walkway would leave you wide open. Up there, you'd be in her line of sight every step of the way."

"So what do you suggest?" asks Beth.

"You can still get out," he says, nodding to himself now. "Through the loading chamber. Once you're through the air-lock, it'll take you straight out into the night."

I consider his suggestion for a moment. I know that I can override the lock on the chamber's exterior shutters at a key-stroke, just as I did with the main door. Even so, I dismiss the idea out of hand. "The pallet stacks might give us the cover we need to reach the chamber," I say, "but as soon as we open up the interior shutters, those guys will be onto us."

"I could keep them busy," suggests Wilson, who draws the keyboard squarely into his possession. "I've been in this job long enough to know how to handle vermin."

37

STALKING THE CAVERNOUS FLOOR, SAMUEL RAMSAY ADDRESSES HIS quarry one more time.

"*Last chance, Hobbes! Your silence suggests you really don't rate Beth's life so highly! Maybe if I told you about the little chat we had on the way here, you'd change your mind about protecting her.*"

The bounty hunter passes through a corridor of bullion cages. He doesn't slow down or even glance at the gold. Whatever it might be worth, even just a bar, he cannot be distracted by the temptation to steal. The girl might have known how to work the black market, but that is not his line of work.

Besides, this is personal now. If the kid was armed, just as Beth warned, Ramsay would've found himself on the wrong side of a gun as soon as the airlock opened. Had he known the truth, he wouldn't have taken such evasive measures to clear the walkway. The bounty hunter casts his mistakes from his mind and resolves to get this job over with quickly.

Despite the low lighting, Ramsay's bearings begin to fall into place. With some kind of closed gallery overlooking the cargo floor, he figures Hobbes and the girl have to be hiding out up there. At an intersection in the cages and pallet stacks, he turns to face the structure in question. Then his eye is drawn to the door below. There it is, at the far end of the floor. Another airlock located within the foot of a central supporting column. Slinging the oxygen tank from one shoulder to the other, the bounty hunter picks up the pace considerably.

"You're a fool, Hobbes. A damn fool!"

In response, with a crackle and a bang, the first electrified needle strikes the floor just in front of him.

Ramsay stops in his tracks. He blinks in disbelief and then rushes for cover as a second blue bolt slices through the gloom. This one ricochets off the cage behind the man, showering him in sparks. Scrambling to the next intersection, he looks up in a bid to locate the source of the attack. What he sees, to his astonishment, is a figure on the walkway. A woman with her hair pulled back and a gun in one hand—but she's not behind the attack. If anything, she's in the same fix as him; vaulting the rail now just as he had, as several electrified needles shoot up through the gantry behind her. As she drops out of sight, Ramsay catches sight of a small cannon underneath the walkway chassis. It's fixed to the structure by some kind of spherical joint. He watches it chase the woman down with another blast, and then lift to fire another volley directly at him.

Sabine-i-Sabah connects with the roof of the cage. She tucks into a roll to absorb the impact and then keeps on going when sparks sizzle and spray beside her. The fall to the floor is less precise, but it's her instinct for survival that drives her now. Cursing to herself, she comes back around the side of the cage. There she finds the cannon in the sightline of her handgun and takes it out with one bullet.

Before the echo from the blast subsides, every other cannon spanning the walkway responds. At once, Sabine finds herself the target from sustained fire. With one needle after another spitting at her, she retreats into the labyrinth.

BETH AND I FACE EACH OTHER INSIDE THE AIRLOCK. WE'RE BOTH wearing breathing apparatus. The masks can't disguise our unease. On the other side, in the main space beyond, all hell has just broken loose. Wilson is behind it. All he asked was that I summon the screen that could restore Cleopatra's aggressive measures, and he took over from there.

It meant that as soon as the assassin and the bounty hunter moved a muscle, the electroshock cannons locked on and opened fire.

"The moment it goes quiet," I remind her, "that's when we make a break." Beth gives me the okay sign, listening with me. As agreed with Wilson, once the cannons have ceased to detect movement, he will disable the censors again so we can attempt to reach the loading chamber. There'll be no guarantee that Sabine and Ramsay are incapacitated, but it's the only means by which Beth can cross the floor free from the very same attack. With no authorization to be here, she risks being targeted by Cleopatra as well.

"If we don't make it," says Beth, as the firing subsides, "I want you to know that I'm sorry. I've messed up more than you can imagine."

"Stop saying that," I tell her. "This may not be the kind of challenge you had in mind, but we're a team again, just like we were in Camp Twilight. Now, are you ready?"

Beth holds my gaze for a moment and then nods. I check that my oxygen tank is functioning and trigger the door release.

Without a flashlight, it is hard to tell if anyone is lurking in the gloom. I cannot see the cannons under the walkway either, but neither do I hear them swivel as we creep out. Gesturing for Beth to follow, I break for the passage directly ahead. I know the layout well enough now to find my way across to the loading chamber. I am also well aware that we are moving among objects of immense value, but now is no time for a guided tour.

I indicate that we will turn at the next pallet, only to see Beth freeze. I spin around just in time to see him. Several blocks ahead, unaware of our presence, Samuel Ramsay crosses our path at an intersection. His attention is fixed on the walkway cannons. I figure he must be preparing to be pinned down once more by another barrage, while also wondering why it has stopped. Certainly it means he doesn't even glance in our direction. I wait a moment after he has slipped from view and continue swiftly on our way. The rack to our left holds a vertically stacked set of huge gilt-edged mirrors. This is my marker. Turning here will bring us directly in line with the delivery chamber.

It also brings me face-to-face with the assassin.

Sabine-i-Sabah reacts with as much surprise as I do. She is quicker at recovering her composure, however, and shows us both a blade.

"Be still!" She narrows her eyes. "And you," she adds, glaring at Beth. "Step aside."

I back up alongside Beth, my breathing rapid inside the mask. I just hope that Wilson is aware of the situation from the control hub. Right now, I would rather face an outbreak of cannon fire than the look of purpose and control in Sabine's eyes.

"If you kill him, then you'll have to take me as well," says Beth.

The assassin takes a step forward, switching the tip of the blade from my throat toward her. As the blade comes back toward me, Beth seizes the advantage. Without warning, she reaches for the rack beside us and hauls one of the mirrors as hard as she can. At once, this vast panel of antique glass slides out on rails. It cuts across the passage, forcing Sabine to step back as it forms a barrier between us.

It also reveals in the mirror's reflection that Samuel Ramsay has picked up on the encounter. For he can be seen charging up the passage behind us.

"This way!" I grab Beth by the wrist and run back to the intersection. Judging by the footfalls, it sounds as if the assassin will make a bid to cut us off at the next block. I can't think why Wilson has yet to reactivate the cannons. One glimpse at the lights moving around his screen would tell him we're in serious trouble. I intend to duck left at the next intersection, only to have Sabine drop into our path. Instead of heading around the rack, she's climbed over the top, and now here she is rising up to her full height once more. We stop in our tracks and take one look back. A moment later, as Ramsay appears at the intersection and levels a baleful gaze on us, I realize we are trapped.

"WHAT NOW?" WHISPERS BETH.

"What now is, I have to make a choice!"

I switch my attention between the bounty hunter and the assassin. Sabine raises one eyebrow at the figure behind us. Samuel Ramsay looks surprised to see her. Judging by the way he sighs and shakes his head, however, she is no stranger to him.

"Only one of us is here to harm you," he says to me. "Do the right thing, Hobbes."

"You swore you'd make Beth suffer," I remind him, keeping my eye on Sabine and the blade in her hand. "How can I trust you?"

Ramsay has no opportunity to reply. I glance over my shoulder to see him draw breath—and that's when the cannons open up.

"Get down!" Beth cries out to me, as the first needles connect with their targets. Unlike us, both Ramsay and Sabine are standing in the intersections between the pallet stacks. It leaves them both within a clear line of fire. I see Ramsay take a hit that knocks him to the floor in a shower of sparks. With Sabine suffering a strike herself, we scramble to our feet.

"Beth, I need to shield you if we're going to get out of this. Do you understand?"

As I speak, both the bounty hunter and the assassin endure a second round from the cannons. Clearly dazed by the onslaught, and with their clothing smoking where they've been struck, they struggle to haul themselves into cover now.

"Let's do it," she replies, as I realize our path is about to be blocked. Beth is the first to move, grabbing a pistol from Sabine's belt. The assassin can be heard groaning and coughing through her mask. She looks up sharply and catches Beth by her foot. I am right behind her and simply push Beth so hard that Sabine loses her grip.

It also means that Beth stumbles into the open.

The cannons respond with several rounds. I see her spin around, dodging both needles through chance as much as quick wits.

"Head for the shutters!" I yell, aware that this involves following a passage directly in the line of fire from the walkway. With no time to reconsider, I urge her to run just ahead of me. I try to fill the space between the pallets, knowing they will not fire at me, but the sensors must pick up on glimpses of Beth. As a result, we find ourselves sprinting from needle after needle. On clearing the passage, directly in front of the loading chamber, she peels to one side and takes cover behind the final pallet cage.

"Go open her up," she says, panting heavily. "I'm good here, and if either of those guys makes a move, I have the gun!"

I rush to activate the panel beside the chamber. The shutter begins to lift, but does so painfully slowly. I glance back at Beth. Judging by the directions in which the cannons are firing, it seems both Sabine and Ramsay have recovered enough to take different paths in pursuit.

"The back of the chamber will be too deep for the cannons to find you!" I shout across at her. "But you'll have to run for it!"

Beth takes one look back, recoils from a needle that spits the length of the passage, and then sprints for the chamber. As she scrambles under the rising shutter, one volley after another strikes behind her. In her desperation to get farther inside the chamber, the pistol in her grasp clips the lip of the chamber and drops to the floor. With no time to recover it, Beth throws herself to the back of the space, curling into a ball as the sparks shower. I follow her in, find the control panel inside, and command the shutter to close. It reacts so slowly that I expect to see Sabine or Ramsay at any moment. Beth is watching out for them too, defenseless now without that gun, and then glances at me as the cannons fall quiet.

The way they cough and stutter into silence tells me something is wrong. It just doesn't sound like the targets are out of sight or incapacitated.

It sounds more like a glitch in the system.

Sure enough, when the shutter stalls just a foot from closing us inside, I know we are in serious trouble.

"Don't fail on us now," I mutter to myself, and attempt to draw down the shutter by hand. Beth is quick to join me. Together, with great effort and to the sound of approaching footfalls, we secure it in place. I waste no time in turning to the control panel. In vain, I attempt to operate the airlock. It does not respond. If the system has gone down, I know that disengaging the exterior shutter is impossible. I find Beth looking at me.

"Technology," she says, finding her breath now. "You can't trust it."

I even think she might show a smile, were it not for the sound of a fist repeatedly thumping the other side of the shutter.

"Get out here!" This is Ramsay, sounding muffled by his mask but furious all the same. *"Get out here now!"*

As he falls quiet, a static crackle comes through the intercom. Then a voice, breaking up some, but clearly belonging to Wilson. *"Carl? Beth? Are you safe?"*

"We could be safer!" I call back. "What's happened?"

"I have no idea. I was trying to find a way to crank up the cannon fire. Now a whole bunch of lights are blinking red on the pyramid."

I look at Beth and tell them both that this confirms what I feared. Cleopatra may have been fail-safe when operating independently. Under human control, especially someone with no experience of operating a supercomputer, the chances of hitting the wrong key are sky-high.

"She'll come back online," I assure Beth. "Right now Cleopatra will be analyzing what's gone wrong and cooking up a fix. We just need to sit tight."

"We don't have so long," she reminds me, and taps at her mouthpiece. "When the tanks run out, we'll all be dead."

I return my attention to the control panel. "Wilson, can you tell me what's happening now?"

"Carl, some of those lights have turned green. The cameras are back up, but . . . wh—!"

Wilson breaks away there, but the channel is still open. It leaves us free to hear every sound from the control hub.

If we can only guess at the struggle taking place, the gunshot is loud enough to be heard without the speaker.

The silence that follows tells me more than I need to know. Even Ramsay pauses in his vicious assault on the shutter. I turn around to face Beth.

"Oh, no." I breathe out into my mask. *"Wilson!"*

"It seems Sabine has more than one gun at her disposal," she replies grimly.

I'm shocked by what I just heard. Shocked and reeling from what it means. For a man has just laid down his life to help us out on this, his final shift.

I am shaken from my thoughts by a crackle across the intercom.

"You can't hide from me, Carl. In fact, it seems your computer is about to betray you too. Those red lights are rapidly switching to green."

Sabine sounds remarkably assured. Unlike Samuel Ramsay, who has evidently found something from the racks to repeatedly batter the shutter. This time he begins to make a dent. Judging by the shape of it, I think he must be attempting to break his way in using a bullion bar.

"We have to get out of here." Beth raises her voice to be heard over the hammering. "Ramsay will have that shutter open whether or not the glitch is fixed."

Still reeling from what's just happened in the control room, I turn my attention to the panel once more. Unlike the one on Ramsay's side, there is no manual override switch. As a safety feature, it gives priority access to anyone on the cargo floor. To my horror, I realize that once Cleo has fixed the glitch he will have complete control.

Just then, despite our vulnerability to the bounty hunter, it's the assassin who reminds me who has overall charge here.

"Hey, Carl." Sabine's voice through the intercom sounds horribly upbeat and playful. *"I see how you unlocked the exterior doors. You left the screen up, idiot. How about I lock them down again? That would mean the main door and . . . oh dear, the shutter between you and the outside world."*

I glance at Beth. "She can't do anything until the system is back online," I tell her under my breath.

"That doesn't make me feel any better about this, Carl." Despite the relative size of this airlock, big enough to transfer the largest items of cargo to and from the main area, it still feels suffocating. I look up and around in desperation. Then I notice Beth turn her attention to the floor. She sighs and shakes her head.

"What?" I ask.

"It's under your nose, Carl!"

When I face Beth once more, having looked for myself, I share her sense of relief. I still feel sick about Wilson, but what we've just found makes me think we now have a slim chance of escaping the same fate.

40

BY NOW, THE BOUNTY HUNTER HAS BROKEN A SWEAT. THE BULLION bar in his grip is more deformed than the shutter. He examines the bar, recognizing that using such a soft metal is getting him nowhere, and tosses it away.

That's when the pistol comes to his attention. The one Beth had dropped in her scramble for the chamber. Calmly Samuel Ramsay collects it from the floor. He takes several paces back, turns to face the shutter, and fires off a round at the lock.

The bullet ricochets into the gloom. To his irritation, the lock remains intact.

"Hobbes, you still have a choice!" he calls out. "I know Sabine. I'm well aware of her history. It's a surprise to find her here, but she won't leave without a picture of your head on a plate. And I mean that quite literally. If you had a buddy in the building, he isn't here anymore. I'm sorry, but I guarantee you that. Her presence changes all the rules. If we don't work together, then we're all as good as dead. So here's what I'm prepared to do. I can get you out of here, with your help, of course, and if Beth means that much to you, I'll do the same for her. No matter what it takes, I'll make sure she escapes with her life. What she does on the outside is your call. She's dead to the military and the CIA, so as far as I'm concerned she can hide herself away. But your part of the deal, my friend, is to give up this damn fool fight to avoid capture."

Samuel Ramsay falls quiet there. He tips his head, waiting for Hobbes to respond. Hearing nothing, he mops his brow and then checks the tank in his shoulder holster. The needle is heading toward empty, which just serves to fire him up again.

"Are you listening, Hobbes?" This time he uses the tank to smash against the shutter. "*Answer* me!"

If the silence enrages him, the sound of cannons swiveling propels him into action. He wheels around, sees the first blue spark crackle at him through the gloom. Ramsay throws himself toward the control panel, narrowly avoiding the needle, and slams his palm against the button to disengage the lock. The second needle strikes him on the shoulder. He cries out as the charge of electricity courses through his body. Despite the impact, with the loading chamber opening at last, he finds the strength to haul himself inside.

What he finds leaves him reeling. Crawling to the back of

the airlock, just out of reach from the cannon's sensors, Ramsay looks around in disbelief.

For Hobbes and the girl are nowhere to be seen. The external shutter remains closed. What's more, he's just heard Sabine inform the pair that she'd lock it down as soon as the system came back online.

For a moment he remains slumped there, panting through the mask. Then a noise turns his attention to the center of the chamber floor. He sees the hatch and immediately moves to flip it open. As he does so, the wheel underneath ceases to turn.

The bounty hunter smiles to himself and prepares to undo the boy's good work.

From the control hub, Sabine-i-Sabah observes the red light shrink and then vanish from the loading chamber. She is standing before the screen, tapping her lips with one finger. Having just watched the lights representing Hobbes and Beth disappear in the same way, she is reminded of frightened rabbits going underground.

"Where are they heading?" she asks.

The security guard is slumped in the chair she has wheeled aside. Wilson's eyes are upturned and without focus, and his mouth hangs slack. Blood is beginning to drip from the upholstery to the floor. Sabine even glances at the corpse, as if hoping he might respond. A moment earlier, on witnessing the last fault light in the pyramid come back online, she carried out her threat to lock down the building. A click of the mouse is all it took for her to turn the perimeter of the wireframe to red. Now, toggling through the documents and reports open on the screen, she finds that her quarry has been very busy indeed. "This one is about me," she tells Wilson, on coming across the file shared with the CIA. "Your boy has done his homework," she adds, nodding to herself now.

The assassin begins to read the file and then appears to remind herself of the task in hand. Returning to the wireframe, she finds the option to view the lower level. The rendering on the screen collapses and then reconfigures to show her the layout under the main area. Instead of a grid, she finds herself looking at a T-shape formation. She frowns, for the red light denoting Samuel Ramsay shows him combing what must be one of three corridors down there.

As for the two other lights, they have disappeared completely.

41

THE ESCAPE HATCH OPENED ONTO A SET OF RUNGS RECESSED INTO THE wall. We had only just dropped through when the system came back online. This I knew for sure, because as soon as I began to spin the wheel to close the hatch above me, the shutters could be heard opening up. On descending frantically to the floor below, we found ourselves looking at a crash door straight ahead, as well as to our left and right. Through the windows in each door, we could see long corridors under strip lights. It felt more like a forgotten hospital wing down here than a cargo warehouse.

With no time to get our bearings, we pushed through the doors in front of us. On each side, we passed storage rooms with biohazard stickers on the glass. Neither of us dared to test the handles. We just kept on moving, picking up the pace on hearing Ramsay clamber down the rungs in pursuit.

Just then I feared we would reach a dead end. If it hadn't been for the glow from a laptop, stationed in the corner of what turned out to be some kind of sample lab, Beth and I would've found ourselves with nowhere to go.

Right now, having slipped inside, Beth checks the dial on her tank. It's clear to me that she doesn't like what she sees.

"By my reckoning," she says, "we only have a couple more minutes before our oxygen runs dry."

"Breathe easy," I say. "We're not finished yet."

The laptop is open on a workbench beside a clipboard and pen. Whoever last used it logged off and simply walked away. Often a system administrator will request all computers to be left running overnight so updates can be installed. This also makes things much easier for hackers like me to gain access and move around. At this moment, however, all I want to do is get *out* of here, which is why I hammer in the user name and password I've set up for myself.

"We're sitting targets," says Beth, facing the window as my fingers fly across the keyboard. "Ramsay will be onto us in no time."

"Not with Cleopatra back on our side," I tell her, as my details are accepted. "I've just accessed her remotely."

To my surprise, on viewing the command screen, I see the menu drop down before I've even clicked on it. At first I think this might be Sabine, at the keyboard in the control hub. There's something about the way the cursor moves so fluidly, however, that makes me suspect Cleo is operating independently here. I watch as it searches rapidly through the command tree, opening dozens of folders and subfolders. When it settles on the option to allow only one user and shuts off access at the control hub, I know for sure that the supercomputer has just acted in my best interests.

I press my finger to the touchpad. Immediately Cleopatra hands over control.

The first thing I do is kill the ambient lighting down here. At once the harsh strips in the corridors go out. I can't do anything about the safety lights, glowing red from inside each storage room. Even if I could, the way Beth shrinks from the door tells me our time has just run out.

"Get down," she hisses through her mask, hurrying back to me. "He's on his way!"

I take the laptop with me, so as not to draw attention through the glass. Crouching behind the lab bench, all Beth and I can do is brace ourselves and listen.

Sure enough, I hear the bounty hunter out in the corridor. By the squeak from the soles of his shoes, he's pausing to peer into the storage rooms. With no time to wait for him to pass, I swivel the laptop around and quietly continue to communicate with Cleopatra. If the monitors are still operating in the control hub, the assassin could well know precisely where we are by the position of our lights on the wireframe layout.

Hunting through the command tree, I find the tracking control folder. I open it up and select an option to modify. To my dismay, the software components inside it are numerous and beyond me. For a moment I just stare at the screen—so intently that a moment passes before I realize Cleopatra has just taken over once more. A box window opens, containing strings of code. I watch her tweak it, close the box, and open the wireframe display. It shows Samuel Ramsay to be right outside the lab in which we're hiding.

In a blink, the green and red lights representing Beth and me are snuffed from view.

I have no time to take in what this tells me about Cleopatra's awareness of our situation. Not when the door opens with a *click*. I glance at Beth, the pair of us holding our breath. It leaves only the sound of Ramsay inhaling and exhaling through his mask. Even when the door closes once more, I dare not move a muscle. All I can do is wait until we hear the footsteps retreat back down the corridor, then crawl out from our hiding place. I return the laptop to the work surface and then glance at Beth.

"Cleopatra won't let us die in here," I assure her. "She's just started second-guessing me."

Beth says nothing for a second. At first she just stares at me like she hasn't heard me right.

"No way!"

"I swear she's predicting the commands I need to make. She knows we're under threat, Beth. I've instructed her to consider us as cargo. So now that we're under attack, I think she's acting to protect us."

"You make it sound like she's coming alive."

"She's learning from experience," I reply. "She's becoming more sophisticated in her strategies to keep us safe from harm."

"So ask her to get us out of here!" Beth urges under her breath.

I wish it could be that easy, but unless she makes another move on our behalf, it's up to me. From the command menu, I ask Cleopatra to list every item of cargo in storage.

"We need to know what's down here," I tell Beth. "If there's anything we can use to our advantage, now is the time to find out."

"If Sphinx stores miracles," she replies, at the window once more, "be sure to tell me."

The list arrives on the screen. It appears to be in order of the date that each item has been signed in. I arrange to view it by floor. What I read draws me closer to the monitor.

"Not again," I mutter to myself, which draws Beth back to me. Just to be sure, I refresh the item order. The list returns exactly the same. "If the hazardous goods are designed for this basement area," I say, "what do you think is in the level underneath?" Beth frowns. I gesture at the screen. "It's listing three levels in total. But all the items stored on the lowest level are showing up as classified." This time I face around to address her directly. "Sphinx has something to hide."

"And only minutes before my air tank runs out," she points out. "I know what's more important to me right now."

As she says this, I see she's beginning to draw breath with some difficulty. The supply from my own tank is also thinning, I realize. Even if she's got through hers a little quicker, it won't be long before I'm also struggling. I know I can restore the oxygen supply from the keyboard. But in doing so, with the bounty hunter and the assassin facing the same predicament, it wouldn't just be us that I'd be keeping alive. Beth is looking at me like she knows I have a choice to make. If I see tension in her face at first, all of a sudden it vanishes. "Don't touch it," she says with conviction now. "We've survived worse things, and I've no intention of making things easier for them. We'll find a way if we hurry."

I return my attention to the laptop. The top-down wireframe shows Ramsay nearing the dispatch chamber once more. I switch to the view of the floor above. It confirms that Sabine has abandoned the control hub for the main floor. Back on the hunt, it seems. She may be heading for the chamber, but her movements are haphazard. I figure the cannons must be holding her up, though we can't afford to assume they'll overwhelm her.

"All I know is that we can't stay here," I say, with mounting frustration.

Beth is watching me intently. "The only way out of this building is up," she says, "and the means to get there is looking way out of bounds."

"Which is why we have to go down." As I speak, I find a way to toggle through a range of different skins for the wire-frame view. I pinpoint one that overlays the power points and another that flags up the water pipes in the ceiling. I feel sure I can uncover one that will show me where the entrance to the level below is located.

When Cleopatra selects it for me, I know we have a closer connection than I could've possibly imagined.

"Did you see that?" Beth looks astonished. She can't argue with me now. On the screen, a room midway between this lab and the chamber has just been highlighted in green. "Let's get going!"

I move to rise, but Beth is noticeably slower. She looks up at me, rising panic in her eyes, and then hauls the oxygen tank from her shoulder. "It's almost out," she says through the mask. "I'm in trouble here, Carl!"

I set the laptop on the bench, my mind made up.

"I'll bring the air back online," I tell her. "We don't have any choice."

I find the command and quickly execute it.

Nothing happens. No change of screen or confirmation window.

I try again. On the third attempt, I realize Cleopatra has overridden the request.

42

THE ASSASSIN CROUCHES WITH HER BACK PRESSED TO A PALLET stack. She's on her way to the dispatch chamber, but it isn't easy. Every time she makes a move, she finds herself under fire once again from the accursed cannons. Earlier, when the keyboard went dead, Sabine muttered that the building was turning against her. Now, as she narrowly misses another needle on breaking for the next block, that seems like a certainty.

It wasn't the cannons that forced her to take such a thought seriously. They had quite evidently been programmed to lock onto anything that moved. She didn't take that personally. What convinced her was the weird moment that had occurred as she prepared to head out across the cargo floor. Without a doubt, before entering the airlock, she had been prevented from accessing the locker containing spare breathing apparatus. As Sabine had reached for the handle, she could've sworn a locking mechanism engaged. No matter what force she applied, it had not budged. And so she had been forced to step out into this oxygen-deprived hangar with what little remained in the tank.

Sabine reaches the stack containing the mirrors. There she draws out each one in turn, before removing a full-length design set within a carved wooden frame. Placing it upright on the floor, she peers at her reflection. Despite the oxygen mask and the worn antique glass, there is a look of grim determination about her.

"Mirror, mirror . . . ," she says to herself, only for her words to trail off with a smile.

This pause for thought appears to energize her. The next time the assassin steps into the line of fire, she does not dive for cover. Instead, facing the cannons, she holds the mirror like a shield. The needles pour forth but cannot touch her now. Insulated by the wooden frame she's holding, and with wave upon wave of sparks crashing over her, she heads directly for the dispatch chamber.

In the level below, stalking the corridors now, Samuel Ramsay reminds himself to take shallow breaths. He checks the needle on the tank. It's just dipped into the red. He reaches for his collar without thinking. The top button is undone, of course. Still, it feels like he's wearing a tie around his throat that needs loosening.

"Damn it," he mutters to himself. "Damn this kid."

Having searched the second of the three corridors, he returns with a quickening pace. So far, Hobbes and his girl have managed to stay one step ahead. It can't last, of course. The air isn't running out on just him alone in this godforsaken tomb. At any moment, the dwindling oxygen will cause panic to kick in. One or the other will break their cover in a bid for air—and that's when he will pounce.

Some of the storage rooms Ramsay had found to be unlocked, but not many. He's tested every door, searching those that opened up, but moving on quickly from the others. Those were bolted for good reason, after all. The range of hazard symbols told him that the environment inside each storage room had to be both unique and critically controlled. From corrosive liquids to carcinogenic powders, the place was like an intensive care unit for dangerous chemicals.

Midway toward the crash doors, however, something halts him in his tracks.

Unmistakeably, it is the sound of a lock disengaging.

He turns to the source. A storage room with a light frosting of ice on the inside. He recalls checking it a moment earlier and finding it to be locked. Frowning now, and braced to fire, the bounty hunter peers through the glass.

At the back of the room, between two wall-mounted cabinets,

he lays eyes on a large digital thermometer. It holds at minus forty-five degrees centigrade. If Hobbes and Beth are hiding out in there, it's no wonder they'd want to make a hasty exit. Had they waited a moment longer, Ramsay might not have heard them, but clearly they were desperate to get out. The temperature would certainly be intolerable in there, but he knew it had to be that low for good reason. For a whole host of explosive chemical substances from benzene to carbon disulfide, anything warmer than minus twenty would cause auto-ignition. In Ramsay's experience of these things, a jar of such stuff pulled out of a freezer would give you a couple of minutes to set in place and get well clear. For a storage facility such as this, keeping the room itself in subzero conditions was a sound precaution. He tests the door, expecting his quarry to fall out shivering. Instead he is met by a blast of cold air and blankets of vapor. He examines the lock cylinder, baffled by the situation, upon which the sound of the crash doors opening gives him no choice but to slip inside.

43

I CANNOT HIDE THIS FROM BETH. SHE WATCHED ME ATTEMPT TO BRING the oxygen back online. She saw the command refused.

"What's wrong?" she asks, some tension in her voice. "Carl, my tank is running out!"

I take one more look at the room Cleopatra has highlighted for us. For whatever reason she has ignored my request for oxygen, I feel sure she has a strategy here. We need to be five doors down, on the opposite side of the corridor. I snap shut the laptop, aware that I am also struggling to breathe inside my own mask.

"Let's get going," I urge Beth. "This way!"

From the position of Ramsay's red marker, I know we are clear to make a break along the corridor. Whatever has caught his attention in one of the other corridors, he hasn't moved for a minute or so. I scramble for the door, only for Beth to drag me back.

"I can't!" She grabs at her mask. *"Can't breathe!"*

"Don't do it! You'll be inhaling nitrogen. It'll stop your heart after just a couple of breaths. Leave it on!"

I grab her by the wrists, desperate to calm her, but it's too late. Her mask is off, a lack of oxygen to the brain kick-starting the flight response. To my horror, I watch Beth searching for air. I rip off my mask and try to press it to her face, but she shakes her head away from it, fighting me senselessly.

"Easy, Beth! Take what's in there!" At first I think the noise I can hear is precious air escaping from my mask. I plead with her for calm once more and then find myself inhaling. I look up and around, and know just what this means. "Look at me!" I demand. "I'm breathing!" At once Beth's eyes meet mine. She looks at me in astonishment, her chest rising and falling now. I draw her attention to the rapid hissing sound. "Cleopatra's *flooding* the place with oxygen."

"Why leave it so late?" asks Beth, clearly shaken still.

"I can only think she has her reasons." I rise to my feet with the laptop and offer her my hand. "So why don't we just work with her and hope she knows what she's doing."

Beth closes her eyes for a beat and then meshes her fingers with mine.

Peering out from the lab, along the length of the corridor, I see some movement through the crash door. A figure climbing down from the dispatch chamber. Sabine, I realize. My heart sinks, and yet her back is turned to us and she still has a couple of rungs to clear.

"Go!" whispers Beth beside me. "It's our last chance!"

Keeping low, I head for the fifth room down. I realize it is becoming warmer down here. It's as if Cleopatra has engaged the heating along with the oxygen. As I move, I see the assassin drop the final few feet, twisting as she does to face the crash door. At first I fear she'll come straight through. Instead she pauses to draw a gun from under her tunic. We're out in the open now, with no time to retreat to the lab, and so all I can do is keep going. I reach the room that Cleo had highlighted on the laptop, pressing myself close alongside Beth. I grasp the handle, but the sound of a hinge squeaking comes from elsewhere.

On the other side of the crash door, I see Sabine has turned her attention to the corridor to our left. With her gun raised, she advances with a target quite evidently in her sights. I test the storage-room door. It's unlocked.

"We should get out of sight," I whisper, and work the handle.

If Beth has time to answer, I do not hear her. For in that instant the silence is obliterated. Preceded by a muffled tinkle of glass, a billowing fireball blows open the crash doors. Where Sabine was standing I see only boiling flames. The noise and the heat are intense, but it happens so swiftly that Beth and I have no time to react. The flames rush toward us through the corridor now, blooming an incandescent green, only to vanish like some malevolent conjuring trick. In a blink it is over. All that is left are blackened surfaces, while an abrasive chemical smell hangs heavily like the smoke.

"Was that a bomb?" Beth is reeling, as am I. The blast has left one crash door twisted and hanging by its lower hinge. The body of Sabine is visible on the floor through there. She is some distance back from where I last saw her. I hear her groan, see her lift her hand to her head. Whatever state she is in, I remind myself that she is here to kill me.

"An explosion like that needed oxygen," I tell her, as we slip out of sight from the fallen assassin. "If Ramsay was behind it, then Cleopatra just timed it to give him a helping hand."

Inside, the storage room looks like all the others. It's furnished with chest freezers and shelving units. Significantly, I think, there are no signs or stickers warning of hazardous material.

Beth turns to face me. She spreads her hands. "So what are we looking for here?"

I look around and then at her feet. She is standing on a large spongelike mat. It looks like the kind of thing designed to handle corrosive spillages. As there is nothing else here of note, it has to be worth investigating.

"Help me," I request, and begin to roll it back.

The hatch underneath is flush with the floor. This one, to my dismay, is protected by a digital combination lock.

"Can you crack it?" asks Beth.

"If I had an hour," I mutter, and glance behind me. Out there, near the dispatch chamber area perhaps, I hear the sound of glass being crushed underfoot. I glance back at the lock and almost laugh out loud when the numbers begin to spin.

"Let's hope she hasn't forgotten the code," observes Beth dryly, as the digits begin to slam into a configuration.

As soon as the bolts retract, we lift the hatch together. What we find appears to be some kind of chamber. A grid of floor lights come on as we peer inside, but such is the depth it's hard to see beyond the foot of the ladder. Out in the corridor, something is clearly occurring behind the damaged crash door. I hear voices and movement, and so we clamber down as fast as we can. I close the hatch behind me, note the combination on the underside screen, and engage the lock. Below, I see Beth standing quite still. It's as if she's just come face-to-face with a wild dog. I drop down beside her and catch my breath.

"Oh, no," I say, laying eyes on the symbol on display everywhere I look. "No *wonder* it's classified!"

Beth turns to face me. "We shouldn't be here," she says. "We really shouldn't be here at all!"

44

THE EXPLOSION HAS BADLY INJURED SABINE-I-SABAH. REGRETTABLY for Samuel Ramsay, it hasn't killed her outright. He walks toward the assassin, watching her struggle to sit up. She's lost her mask in the blast, he notes. Not that either of them needs one any longer. As soon as he heard the oxygen rush through the vents, Ramsay knew he could use it to his advantage. Not only did it mean he could discard his breathing apparatus, it turned every flask in the freezer into a potential bomb. In the face of that detonation, Sabine is lucky to have escaped with her life. Her clothing is scorched and shredded in places, while her neck, cheek, and hands have suffered some burns. She sees him coming and attempts to crawl away.

"Triethylborane," he says, crunching through the shattered glass remains of the flask he lobbed at her. "If you want to fire up a high-speed jet engine, this is the stuff to use. The American air force uses it to kick-start the Blackbird spy plane. It's highly flammable and guaranteed to ignite spontaneously at minus three degrees, as you've just found out to your cost."

"You aren't here for me." Sabine is struggling to reach her handgun, blown from her grasp by the blast.

Casually the bounty hunter swipes it away with his foot. She watches the weapon skitter across the floor and drops her head.

"And there's no reward to be claimed from taking my life," he reminds her. "It's over for you, Sabine. You lost out this time. It might not please your paymasters, but that's just how it is. Now let me go hunt down the boy and get out of this hellhole. I'm really beginning to sweat in here."

For a moment the pair regard each other in silence. There is an air of animosity between them as well as some respect. Then Ramsay mutters something more to himself about the air-conditioning and turns for the crash doors.

A moment later, as he walks away, he stumbles like someone who has stepped off a curb without realizing it's there. Samuel Ramsay's left knee sinks as he twists around, a look of astonishment and pain contorting his face, before dropping to the ground.

"It's far from over," growls the assassin, having just drawn a hunting knife from the webbing under her tunic and flung it with precision. The handle is all that's visible now, square between Ramsay's shoulder blades. "Though I can only speak for myself."

With a struggle, Sabine-i-Sabah picks herself up from the floor. For a moment she remains on her hands and knees, gathering her strength before rising to her feet. She looks down at the bounty hunter. He's lying at an awkward angle, making efforts to grasp the blade embedded in his upper back. When he does succeed and pulls it free, his roar of pain resounds through the corridors. On settling again, panting heavily, he turns his head and finds her looking at him impassively. "You're bleeding heavily," she observes, on noting the dark pool spreading underneath him. "That has to be a major artery all cut up inside you now."

"Shoot me," he says with some effort, clearly aware of the severity of his injuries. "Finish this, Sabine."

With a grimace, the assassin collects the pistol he kicked away earlier. She levels it at him once more, her aim somewhat unsteady, and then thinks better of it. "I should save the bullet," she says, picking her way around him. "If you're still alive when you hear gunfire, you'll know I got your man."

45

THE SYMBOLS ARE UNMISTAKABLE. BETH KNOWS JUST WHAT THEY spell: trouble. I would expect to find this kind of thing on display around the perimeter of a nuclear power plant, perhaps. Not here. Not inside a freight storage facility for an international airport.

"Whatever this is," she says finally, "it's radioactive."

It's as if we've discovered a burial chamber, but with transportation cylinders in the surrounding racks instead of coffins. Each one displays the warning symbol, along with a serial number.

"I can see why Sphinx has gone to such lengths to keep this under wraps," I say. "They keep some hot cargo down here. Is it even legal to move it around by air?"

"That's not our concern now." Beth is still facing the cylinders. "I just need to know why Cleopatra wanted to show it to us." She pauses there and looks around. "There's no way out from here, after all."

I set the laptop on the floor in front of the cylinders and open it up.

"Let's find out," I say, on accessing the command screen. "She'll have a strategy here."

As I speak, a second window pops up. It displays the ambient temperature control throughout the building. I note that the digits in the thermometer are continuing to rise. "The heat is on," I say, "but why is she making it so uncomfortable?"

I switch to the wireframe for the underground level. I see one red light stationary at the point where the three corridors meet, while the other is located in the room directly above us. Whoever it is must know we are down here. I ask Cleopatra to show me all the locks engaged on this level. I just want to be sure I have secured the hatch. Instead, ignoring my request, she highlights the chest freezers in each storage room. Then she numbers them in turn, shrinking the wireframe a little to display a corresponding list that shows their fixed temperatures. These range from minus ten to minus three hundred.

"What's going on?" asks Beth, and then gasps as one by one Cleopatra switches off each freezer.

For a moment we watch the numbers replaced by the word *offline*. Midway through the list, I turn to Beth. Any horror in my expression is easily matched in hers.

"By warming this building, she's rigging it to explode," I say in a whisper. "The chemicals in those chests are highly volatile. We all saw what happened to Sabine just now. Shutting down the freezers leaves everything at the mercy of the ambient temperature. My God, Beth. If it all goes up, it's going to create a *firestorm!*"

Beth snaps her attention toward the cylinders. I know just what's on her mind. With a fire raging for a long time in an enclosed space like Sphinx, nothing would withstand the heat.

"What kind of idiot would store radioactive and flammable materials in the same building?"

"An idiot who believes technology is one hundred percent fail-safe when humans are involved in the system," I tell her. "The kind of people who make my work possible, though right now I'm questioning the wisdom of messing with a supercomputer before I truly understood what I was doing. This is one sophisticated strategy she's devised, but there's madness in her methods now."

Just then, we hear a mechanical thud above us. It resounds through the corridors, like the sound of many locks disengaging. I glance at the laptop screen. Beneath the list of all the freezers that have just been shut down, I read confirmation from Cleopatra that she's just popped the lids.

"She's insane!" Beth declares, ignoring my awkward apology

for getting her into this. "If this place burns down, it could contaminate the area for miles around!"

My guts twist at the thought. Feeling a terrible sense of responsibility now, I consider everything I have learned about Sphinx Cargo. Then there were the boasts and claims by Willard Thorn about how the structure could withstand every kind of assault. Even the architect's plans suggested a modern-day fortress.

Not just on the outside, I realize with a jolt, but also on the *inside*. If Sphinx could survive an apocalyptic event, it could certainly contain one too.

"She's doing it to protect us," I say. "Cleopatra sees the current threat to our safety as being sky-high. What she's doing is responding in kind."

"And this is an appropriate measure? Carl, she won't just kill us all. She could wipe out thousands! She might be a supercomputer, but no amount of technology can simulate the heart!"

Beth is silenced by the muffled sound of an explosion. On the wireframe, one of the storage rooms in the right-hand corridor begins to blink.

"It's started," I say, with no time to explain what I believe she is doing. "We have to get out of here."

"How?"

On the screen, I note that the red light that has been motionless in front of the dispatch chamber is now nowhere to be seen. Meantime, the second light is moving rapidly toward the room where the explosion just occurred. I figure this one has to be Sabine. Ramsay has demonstrated some understanding about chemicals, as his attack on the assassin proved to me. Anyone with an awareness of what has just caused the explosion would not be hurrying to investigate. Like us, they would be clamoring to get away.

I watch the red light turn into the right-hand corridor. There it slows to a halt. I imagine Sabine has just laid eyes on a scene of devastation: blown-out glass, flames licking through the frames, and smoke spreading across the ceiling. The first of many explosions, I fear, all of which can only feed the fire. We watch the light continue to move closer. This won't keep her distracted for long, I realize. If we're going to make a break, it has to be now. What I need to know from Cleopatra is the move she expects us to make. We're in her hands now, after all.

"We need a status report," I say, and hurriedly access the command menu. Once again, however, the supercomputer second-guesses me.

"What does it say?" asks Beth, as line after line of information tracks across the screen.

"The sprinkler system has been taken offline," is the first thing I read out loud, though it's the information string in bold that draws my attention. There it is, midway down, clearly out-lined for me. "Three minutes from now," I report, "she's sealing the fire doors to the backup generator on both the upper and lower levels."

I stop there and stare at Beth. Under any other circum-stances, I would've kicked myself for not investigating this part of the system properly. Had I ventured down the spiral staircase, instead of simply peering from the top flight, I would've known a door existed that connected this level to the gallery. "That's our way out," I tell Beth. "But we have to move fast, because I believe she's taking steps to save herself here."

Beth is reading the report as I speak. She gestures at the screen.

"The generator room is a hyperlink. Click on it, Carl."

Immediately we're taken back to the wireframe view. There is Sabine, her positional light closing in on the fire in the left-side corridor. At the far end of the corridor to the right, however, a door has been highlighted in green. I snap the laptop shut.

"Get going!" I yell, along with the code for the hatch as I take to the ladder behind Beth.

Frantically she punches in the digits. The hatch remains sealed. On the second failed attempt, Beth looks back at me with sheer panic in her eyes.

"She's locked us in! Carl, we're going to *die* here!"

I'm at a loss to think why Cleo would do this. Ever since Ramsay appeared on the monitors, she's been operating to protect me as cargo. Now, it seems, she's turned against me. I stare at Beth, desperate now for some kind of explanation.

And there, in a blink, I find it.

"It's you," I say, aghast. "Cleopatra is after *you*!"

Beth looks nervous all of a sudden. She breaks from my gaze, just for a moment, and sighs when she finds it once more.

"Ramsay wasn't holding me hostage," she confesses. "I'd arranged to sell the gold bar to a contact, just as you guessed, and when I arrived he was lying in wait for me. He wanted to know how to find you. Said he'd turn me over to the CIA if I didn't comply. Thinking on my feet, I cut him a deal. I agreed to take him to Sphinx, and in return I asked him to get me inside."

I say nothing for a moment. I am stunned to hear it, but somehow unsurprised.

"So when I ambushed Ramsay on the gantry, that was the last thing you needed."

"I'm sorry," she says. "He swore no harm would come to you."

I press my palm to the crown of my head, struggling to think. I feel betrayed, but I'm also angry at myself because I should've known better. And yet despite what Beth's revealed, my instinct for survival tells me we have to keep working together.

"None of this explains why Cleopatra would want to take you out," I say. "Unless—"

I am stopped there by what Beth has just produced from a pocket. She opens up the velvet pouch and reveals the biggest diamond I have ever seen.

"The cage I hid behind while you opened up the dispatch chamber . . . ? I couldn't help myself."

I'm thinking about Cleopatra as she tells me this—and now everything makes sense.

"Pass it to me," I urge her. "In my hands she won't consider it to be stolen. I'm cargo, just like the rock." Beth returns the diamond to the pouch, only to hesitate and look back at me. "Give it up!" I yell. "I'm not going to lose my life in here because of a rock!"

This time she drops the pouch into my hands and then punches in the code for the lock once more.

The hatch opens with a *click*.

46

TORTUROUSLY, SAMUEL RAMSAY DRAGS HIMSELF TOWARD THE RUNGS
beneath the dispatch chamber.

The floor is covered in debris. He is very pale, perspiring in beads, and his bearded face knots as he crawls. He leaves a smeared trail of blood behind him. A moment earlier, an explosion from the right-side corridor roused him from unconsciousness. With the assassin nowhere to be seen, he summoned what strength was left in his body and began the short but agonizing passage out of here.

For whatever caused another cylinder to detonate, it will not be the last. Not with the air temperature ramped up so high. The place has become a pressure cooker. That's how the bounty hunter sees it now. A pressure cooker with a chemical stew beginning to bubble and boil.

At the foot of the ladder, Ramsay hears footsteps behind him. He drops his head and lets his body go limp. With nothing at hand to defend himself, all he can do is play dead. Judging by the lightness of foot, he is sure Sabine is approaching. If she puts a bullet through the back of his skull, he thinks to himself, he might just consider it an act of kindness.

The bounty hunter hears her slow down, considering him, perhaps. He tightens his eyes, preparing himself, only for her to push through the crash doors into the right-side corridor.

Summoning his last reserves, Samuel Ramsay hauls himself onto the rungs and begins to clamber for the dispatch chamber. His footing slips on several occasions, the rungs slick with his own blood, and yet his teeth remain gritted in determination. He pushes through the hatch, inviting a spray of needles from the electroshock cannons up on the walkway. Once again, every strike fails to reach deep enough inside the chamber. The bounty hunter is showered in sparks as he drags himself as far back as he can. Struggling for breath now despite the oxygen-replenished atmosphere, he looks more like a wounded animal who has just found someplace to die.

Sabine-i-Sabah picks her way through the debris caused by this second explosion. Just now, before the bang drew her attention, she was sure Beth and Hobbes had taken refuge beneath that hatch. Then again, if a level existed below this one, perhaps they had surfaced over here. With her endgame in mind, she checks that the cell phone and her secondary blade are still stowed in the webbing inside her tunic.

Wherever her quarry is hiding out, nobody can stop her from sending through the image so badly sought by her pay-masters. Even if this should be her final job, she thinks, it would be a noble way to go.

With her pistol primed, the assassin peers through the shat-tered window frame. At the back of the room, one of the freezers is ablaze. The smoke rising off it is thick and black, and though it's beginning to fill the room, it's quite clear that her prey is not here. With no hatch in the floor, she considers checking the remaining storage rooms beyond. Something caused this explo-sion, after all.

What stops Sabine is the sound of footfalls.

She circles around, sees her quarry wheel through the smashed remains of the crash doors opposite, with Beth sprint-ing close behind. Hobbes glances back, outstretching his hand to the girl. Whether he notes the assassin's presence is uncertain. All Sabine knows is that they can't ignore the bullets as she levels her aim and opens fire.

47

WITH SECONDS TO GO BEFORE CLEO CLOSED OFF THE FIRE DOOR, I bolted from the storage room with Beth close behind. Ignoring the blood on the floor, the debris, and the smoke, we sprinted into the left-facing corridor. I could see our target at the far end. An exit that should be closed at all times but that had clearly been sprung for us by the supercomputer. Just then I turned to check that Beth was still with me.

And that's when the gunfire opened up behind us.

"Keep going!" I yell at her now as the bullet sings the length of the corridor. "Run, Beth!"

Our hands meet and I cling to her tightly, ducking on instinct as another shot rings out. I figure the smoke must be making it hard for Sabine to get a bead on us. We still have some way to go, however. I brace myself for the next round, sure that a bullet will find us, but that isn't what causes us both to throw ourselves to the floor.

It is the explosion from the storage room we've just cleared. One that blows out the windows with a roar.

I feel the shock waves as I hit the ground. The blast shakes the building to its foundations, battering my ears once more. I look up and around, dazed by what has happened. A moment later, some distance behind us, another storage room goes up with staggering ferocity.

"Are you okay?" Beth is picking herself up. She offers me her hand. I yell at her that I am fine, though my hearing sounds like a radio off frequency.

"We're going to make it!" I assure her, scrambling for the fire door now. The smoke and dust is intense, and I can't ignore the crackle of flames gathering strength. At any time, as the temperature climbs, I just know we can expect more explosions. Sure enough, as we race into the generator room one after the other, an almighty eruption goes off in our wake.

"Don't stop, Carl!"

I have paused only to turn and see if we are being followed. We leave the corridor in ruins. Tongues of fire are licking from shattered doors and windows. The floor is littered with debris, and the air is thick with smoke. I see no sign of Sabine, however. Something even tells me I should go back for her. I try to shoulder open the fire door once more, only for it to force me back as Cleo chooses that moment to lock down.

"What are you waiting for?" Beth's voice brings me round to face the interior. I find she's taken to the spiral staircase already, which she continues to climb at full pace now. The generator occupies the space inside. It's towering and cylindrical, clad in pipes, valves, dials, and switches. As I race to catch Beth, I realize from the growing rumble that it's begun to power up.

If Cleopatra is orchestrating her survival, it seems we are a beat behind her. For as soon as Beth makes the top flight, the fire door up there begins to close. I see her seize the handle, wrestling to stop the mechanism. I slam my foot in the gap, and together we force it open just enough for us each to pass through. I am last out, and as soon as I remove my weight, it snaps shut like some predatory jaw.

"Cleo isn't going to stop for us now!" I say, and rest my hands on my knees for just a moment. "She's calling all the shots."

"But she considers you to be cargo," replies Beth. "She should be protecting you at all costs!"

"For some reason," I say, "she's begun taking steps to protect *herself* over everything else."

Beth turns to the central control room. "Surely we can switch her off?"

She doesn't wait for a response, sprinting instead for the door. The locks are engaged, she finds, and remain that way even when she steps back and kicks at it repeatedly. As she does so, I am reminded not just of the looming pyramid inside but also of the body on the floor. What happened to Wilson came out of nowhere. I also realize that without his encouragement I would've simply surrendered to the bounty hunter. Watching Beth give up on the door, I know that I owe him my life. I think about his manuscript, unfinished in the monitoring room. Now I know how his story ends. I just hope ours isn't about to cease with such violence.

"Don't waste the time," I say, running to join her now. I gesture at the airlock in the center of the gallery. "Cleopatra is battening down the hatches to see this storm through. Beth, she has every intention of surviving it—but unless we move, we're toast!"

48

THE AIRLOCK IS OPEN ON BOTH SIDES OF THE POD. WE'RE FREE TO breathe, I realize. I just don't know whether Cleopatra has ramped up the oxygen to give us a chance or to feed the flames. Across the cargo floor, smoke hangs over the pallets in slashed veils. I look to the dispatch chamber and see flames jabbing from the hatch.

"What about the cannons?" asks Beth.

I look up and around. Despite the fact that the crackling, crashing, and popping from the level below is sounding more like a ship's hold in a storm, an eerie calm holds forth here.

"You'd be under fire by now," I say. "I'm guessing the smoke is obscuring the motion sensors."

Behind us, we hear the airlock closing.

"Well, I guess we're going to have to put that to the test," mutters Beth. "There's no way back now."

"Cleo's fireproofing the gallery like she just did with the

backup generator," I say. "Whatever I've done to rewire her objectives, she's not prepared to sacrifice herself here."

"So what are we waiting for?"

As Beth glances at me, a colossal explosion from the lower level rocks the building to the rafters. A plume of flames licks out of the dispatch chamber, but it's the shock waves from the blast that cause the walkway to twist and sway. Grasping the railings to stay on our feet, we hear several suspension wires snap away from the structure. At once, the walkway tilts and buckles. In turn, with fewer wires supporting the weight, yet more begin to fail.

"We're not going to make it!" Beth shouts as bolts from a central section of the walkway wrench away. *"Carl!"*

In the wake of this last explosion, fires have broken out down below. I see several pallets of canvas frames ablaze. I also detect movement in the shadows.

"We have to give it a shot, Beth. Right away!"

Together, without another word, we race across the fracturing walkway. Whatever blew up in the level below just now has given way to a low, muted roar. It sounds like the furnace I imagine it is becoming down there. Even if the cylinders that contain the radioactive material are made from lead, I figure Cleopatra is calculating exactly how to stoke the flames until they melt.

Underfoot, it feels like we're trying to cross a rope bridge.

Footplates sag and switch as more wires lose the fight to support this giant structure. One snaps away as Beth passes by. She screams and flinches as it snakes into the gloom.

I grab hold of her, desperate now, but with the sudden twist in the walkway that there's no way we can stay upright. With some violence we are thrown to one side. I lose my grip on the laptop, watch it drop away, but I'm more concerned that we don't follow. We grasp at the handrail, holding on with all our might as the central section fails and bursts apart.

With a scream of metal and bolts shearing, the walkway breaks in two. Each section yawns toward the cargo floor, tipping steeply enough for us to lose our footing. Beth swings right into me. The collision causes us both to lose our hold on the rail, just as the fractured end of the walkway crashes between the pallets directly below. I feel myself sliding, tumbling together with Beth, reaching in vain at twisted metal and then coming to rest in a heap on the floor. The impact knocks my breath away. The smoke down here is thinner, but the crackle of flames sounds very close by indeed. Beth is first to pick herself up. I hear her coughing as I drag myself into a sitting position. Then she gasps. I look up with a start.

In that moment, any way out feels a million miles from here.

49

"YOU PUT ON QUITE A SPECTACLE, HOBBES. NOW IT'S MY TURN."

Sabine emerges from behind a pallet. The livid burns striping her neck and collarbone cannot distract me from the intensity of her glare. In one hand she brandishes a blade, in the other a pistol. With her thumb, she clicks back the hammer. Her aim is a little shaky, and though she glares at Beth, the weapon is clearly directed at me.

"I need this picture," she says. "It's worth more to me now than anything here."

I see her finger tighten around the trigger.

"That can't be true!" says Beth. "The items in here are priceless. Take what you want and get out while we still have a chance!"

"It is time," she replies, though the report from her gun muffles her final declaration to me.

"Carl!"

I hear Beth, but it is too late to react. All I can do is turn to meet her eyes and then blink in confusion.

For the bullet has gone wide. We turn to the assassin. She is staring at me in some bewilderment. Her mouth forms words, but she makes no sound. With her expression widening into shock, she turns her attention to her midriff. I see the tip of a knife protruding from there just as she does. A cry dies in her throat.

She looks up at me, blood trickling from her mouth now, and promptly drops the pistol. Beth moves toward her, halting cautiously as the assassin falls to her knees. With a final sigh, and her eyes back on me for a moment, Sabine collapses facedown at our feet.

"Didn't I tell you I'd take care of you?"

Behind her, equally battered and blood-soaked, stands Samuel Ramsay. I hadn't seen him run the hunting knife through Sabine. He turns his attention from the body to the blade still in his grasp. A moment later, it clatters to the floor.

I climb to my feet, standing beside Beth now, and stretch out my hand. "Come with us," I offer, for he's clearly in a very bad way. "Unless we help each other, we're all dead."

He smiles faintly, his face ghostly pale, and shakes his head. "You took the words right out of my mouth. Too late now, though. This is one bounty I'm gonna have to let go." He stops there, slumping like a drunk against the pallet behind him. "Get out of here," he says, waving us away. "Go now!"

I glance at Beth and then look up at the remains of the walkway. The end of the section we had failed to reach looms above us. It's too high to reach, though cables drape from the underside like jungle vines. Another explosion from below us brings my focus back to Ramsay. Through the smoke I see him regarding me. Without a word, he grasps a bunch of cables. Pulling them tight with both hands, and growling over the sound of creaking metal, the bounty hunter draws down the jagged edge of the walkway.

"Come with us," I plead, as Beth climbs a pallet rack and hauls herself up. "If we can get out in one piece, surely that's reward enough?"

The bounty hunter grunts and grits his teeth. "Just go before I change my mind."

"I won't do that!" I insist, sounding frantic now. "I don't care who you are. I won't abandon anyone!"

Maybe he doesn't hear me, but his silence is final. Looking at his condition, I realize I am leaving a dying man behind. As I reach up to follow Beth on this frantic, desperate climb, I know that all Samuel Ramsay is asking for here is the space to prepare for the end.

50

HAND OVER HAND, FOOT OVER FOOT, I RACE TO FOLLOW BETH.

The crashing and creaking from the level below does not stop. The heat is building rapidly, while my lungs feel like they're being scoured of air. Near the top, however, another sound begins to rise up through the din. The pitch is so high I barely hear it, but as the volume rises, I begin to grimace. Vaguely, I remember Wilson telling me that Cleopatra could trigger a noise at a frequency that could force out the rats. I am exhausted, weak, and shaken through, but it's so intense on my ears that my instinct is to get away. If for some reason she considers me to be vermin now, I don't doubt she could exterminate us. I would just like to think at this moment in time that perhaps it's her way of driving us out.

Standing on the fractured platform in front of the airlock, I find Beth reaching down for my hand. She's also clearly tortured by the noise.

"We still have time," I say breathlessly. "If Cleopatra's let those cylinders blow already, she'd have sealed the building!"

As I find my footing and rise up next to Beth, I can't help but turn for one final look across the cargo floor. Fires are burning from one corner to the next, but it isn't just the pain in my eardrums that causes us to turn and run. It's the deep, unending roar from the lower level. The final moment before an apocalypse occurs within these walls.

The airlock opens onto the atrium without either of us having to press a single button. As we hurtle for the main doors, I really think we have made it. But the security pod fails to unclasp as we approach. In desperation I thump my fists at it.

"The diamond!" Beth yells. "Get rid of it!"

I had completely forgotten I still had it in my possession. Without a moment to lose, I fling the pouch from my pocket. As it hits the floor, the diamond skids free. I look up at Beth. She regards it with a torn expression, only to be drawn by the sound of the pod sliding open.

"We're clean!" I cry as the main door beyond clicks ajar for us. *"Move!"*

Together we sprint into the open. Cold, damp air hits my face like a balm. I hear the door close automatically behind us, bringing silence to our ears, but we do not stop there. Dawn is on the cusp of breaking. The streetlamps are still glowing, but the industrial neighborhood is waking up to another working day. It feels like we've stumbled into a different world. One with a glimmer of light on the horizon.

"Stop, Carl! Just stop for a moment!" Beth draws to a standstill. I turn to face her, panting hard and lost for words. She holds my eye for a moment. "When I showed up with Ramsay," she says, "I still had the gold bar. He busted me before I'd sold it. The whole way here I kept it in my shoulder bag, out of sight and out of mind."

I tip my head, confused. "So where are you heading with this?"

Beth grins wickedly and beckons me back toward the main door. For one insane second I think she's returning to the lobby. Instead she makes for one side of the semicircle of concrete crash bollards, there to protect the entrance. Crouching briefly, she collects a bag from behind the one closest to the building. When she hurries back, I shake my head and smile despite myself.

"I see where you're heading now," I say, as we hurry across the parking lot.

"Correction," Beth replies. "Where *we're* heading. If you're willing. You helped me out just now, and despite everything, I can still help you. My contact will be happy to cash this now that Ramsay no longer poses a threat, and that'll get us far and away from here." As we move, she unzips the bag to show me the bar inside. She also catches my eye and notes that I'm less than impressed. "It's a bitter pill, Carl, but we rely on each other."

"Can we discuss this elsewhere?" I say, and glance anxiously over my shoulder.

Beth doesn't respond, because a muffled boom occurs from within the building. It must be significant, I think, because we feel this one through the ground beneath our feet. Somewhere nearby, the tremor even triggers a car alarm. It's enough to cause us to stop and turn around.

"We're looking at a disaster about to happen," she says as we hurry away. "Once that radioactive material gets into the air, it could spread for miles around!"

"Cleopatra has other plans," I assure her. "I have a feeling she won't allow Sphinx to burn down. It just doesn't compute in her world."

Looking at the building now, it's hard to believe that a toxic inferno is burning within. There's no sign of external damage. Nor can I detect a sound from inside any longer. I am certain the soundproofing remains intact. I just question if there's anything to hear. For even if those cylinders have failed in the heat, releasing their contents into the air, it would only take a moment for Cleo to fill the place with nitrogen and deprive the fire of its fuel.

I am about to share my thoughts with Beth, but the sound

of a vehicle turning into the parking lot seizes our attention. Quickly we move toward the side wall, but not before we're spotted.

"Who's this?" asks Beth.

"A colleague," I say, as Sara Sinclair pulls up in her usual space.

She kills the engine and looks through the windshield at me questioningly. There's no way she'll be returning to her desk for decades. Even so, I figure she won't lose out financially. If I'm right about the real purpose of this freight cargo outfit, the players behind the operation will need to cover this up at every level. The hush money could even see her right for life.

"Is something wrong?" asks Sara, stepping from the car. "How did you even get out?"

"With a little help from a friend," I tell her, as we continue to back away.

"Who are you talking about?" Beth whispers to me, though I choose not to answer. Later I will tell her that I believe I have finally come to understand Cleopatra's strategy here. Yes, we could've paid for it with our lives, but having relied on our wits to escape, she is now in a position to stay with us for the long haul. What troubles me, however, is that there's no way she could've known we'd make it out. Quite simply Cleo took a risk, which is both astonishing to me and deeply frightening. It means there's no way now that I could ever feel entirely safe in her hands. She may have permitted this one item of cargo to leave her confines, but by taking such a reckless gamble she acted more like a *human* than a supercomputer, and I could never fully rely on that.

For now, though, and so long as I stay smart, it's good to have her onboard.

"I think it's fair to say my work here is done," I say to Beth, as Sara locks up her car while looking at us with some suspicion. Having studied my exit routes before I joined Sphinx Cargo, I gesture at a wall behind us. Beyond the truck bay on the other side, I know a shortcut leads to the airport apron road. Right now, that's our path to freedom. As we continue to retreat, I glance up at the brightening sky. For coming in over the trading estate is the first of the jumbo jets. The noise is immense as the plane sweeps overheard, so low it looks just seconds from disaster. I turn to Beth. See her watching it too.

"Let's get out of here," I say, and raise a hand in farewell to the baffled-looking receptionist. "It's high time we took off."

51

ON REQUEST, WILLARD THORN RISES TO HIS FEET BEFORE THE assembled personnel. He shoots his cuffs and clears his throat. To the military staff, department representatives, and their many aides, he looks like a man about to present a rock-solid report. Instead, on taking a breath, he appears quite lost for words.

After a long, awkward silence, it's the chair of this emergency meeting who puts him out of his misery.

"You call yourself security director for Sphinx Cargo, Mr. Thorn. But exactly who is in charge of the present situation? Is it you, or as we understand things, some goddamn computer?"

The woman who has tabled the question can barely suppress her rage. As assistant to the president for national security affairs, Pamela Boyers sits upright, awaiting a response. For whatever

258

she hears is going to have to be relayed to the top.

Thorn drops his gaze to the papers in front of him. "Cleopatra is a state-of-the-art super—"

"We *know* this," she cuts in, making every effort to remain calm. "We are well aware of how many millions of dollars went into her creation, because it hammered the department budgets. But, hey! Given the nature of the cargo we were flying out, we felt it was a worthy investment. A way to call in our favors at a later date. Mr. Thorn, do you have any idea what a strain this has placed on our relationship with the British government? We entered into a classified arrangement to remove radioactive waste safely from their shores, and awarded Sphinx the contract. Now, thanks to Carl Hobbes and your incompetence, we've left them with their own private *Chernobyl*!"

Boyers's volcanic outburst is met by silence. Willard Thorn stares at her, blinking in astonishment. When he speaks again, he does so very quietly, as if hoping it might cool the atmosphere.

"Ma'am, this is very different from a nuclear power plant meltdown. The building can safely contain the contamination. Sphinx Cargo is effectively a sarcophagus now. A burial chamber, if you will. There is no way a single particle can escape."

"Unless your computer elects to throw open her doors," she retorts, "or leak it into the water waste."

"She won't do that." Thorn leafs through his papers. This time he draws out a document. A printout of an e-mail addressed to him. His cheeks begin to flush. "So long as we keep to the terms of the deal."

Across the table from Thorn, one of the high-ranking military members present shakes his head to himself.

"A pact made with a PC," he says, almost growling.

"A supercomputer," Thorn counters protectively, and then addresses Boyers directly. "It's in programming language," he explains. "If/then scenarios. That kind of thing."

"*If* you screw up, *then* you pay the price," the military guy mutters. He glances at the figure beside him, a CIA officer wearing oval glasses. He doesn't react in any way. Just stares at his briefing papers. Whether or not he heard the comment, there's clearly some weight on his mind.

"Basically, ma'am," continues Willard Thorn, "Cleopatra has made one very simple request. All she asks is that we leave the solar panels uncovered. The fire melted the network power cables, but she has a backup generator running in there. A solar-powered generator."

"And that's it?" Pamela Boyers looks unconvinced. "Why?"

"So she can draw down juice to continue with her work," he replies.

"But everything inside Sphinx Cargo is unrecoverable. God

knows the insurance payout is going to be *grotesque*. Add on the compensation to keep Sphinx's staff and clients quiet, and . . ." She pauses there and pinches the bridge of her nose. "I'm beginning to get a headache here, Mr. Thorn. Why don't you level with us all? Exactly what kind of work does your computer have in mind?"

"Unauthorized work, ma'am." Willard Thorn reaches for his tie knot. He glances across at the man from the military. Then at the CIA guy, who is now giving Thorn his full attention. In the face of such hostility, it's clear Thorn is preparing to reveal what he knows. At the same time, one of the female aides to Pamela Boyers has been drawn to the door. There she offers her ear to a man wearing an open-necked shirt and an identity tag. The aide nods at what she's hearing. When she turns around, she finds the room waiting for her.

"Ma'am, we're picking up reports that Carl Hobbes has surfaced in Sri Lanka. He's operating *right now* from a laptop repair shop in downtown Colombo."

"Is this a visual sighting?" Willard Thorn is the first to break the silence.

"It's better than that, sir." The aide looks elated all of a sudden. "It's a communication from the suspect himself to his father in the UK."

"An e-mail?"

"Coded, of course, and sent to his secretary at work, but we have Hobbes Senior covered."

Willard Thorn bows his head. Boyers is the first to note it.

"Is there something you need to tell us?"

"Carl Hobbes did not send that e-mail," he says with conviction. "It's a fabrication. I would suggest the first of many for years to come. If I'm brutally honest, it's more sophisticated than I anticipated. But then I have to say I expect nothing less from the perpetrator. Over time, this operation to keep the boy at large is highly likely to continue evolving. It may even exceed anything we could predict."

"You seem quite sure of this, Mr. Thorn."

The security director meets her gaze, resigned now to one simple fact.

"Ma'am, the hacker has an apprentice now. Her name is Cleopatra."

Pulse It

Did you love this book?

Want to get access to the hottest books for free?

Log on to simonandschuster.com/pulseit
to find out how to join,
get access to cool sweepstakes,
and hear about your favorite authors!

Become part of Pulse IT and tell us what you think!

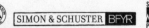

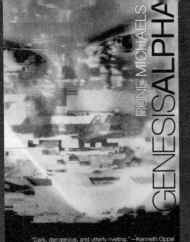

Imagine you and your best friend head out west on a cross-country bike trek. Imagine that you get into a fight—and stop riding together. Imagine you reach Seattle, go back home, start college. Imagine you think your former best friend does too. Imagine he doesn't. Imagine your world shifting. . . .

jennifer bradbury SHIFT

★ "Fresh, absorbing, compelling."
—*Kirkus Reviews*, STARRED REVIEW

★ "Bradbury's keen details about the bike trip, the places, the weather, the food, the camping, and the locals add wonderful texture to this exciting first novel. . . ."
—*Booklist*, STARRED REVIEW

"The story moves quickly and will easily draw in readers."
—*School Library Journal*

"This is an intriguing summer mystery."—*Chicago Tribune*

"*Shift* is a wonderful book by a gifted author."—teenreads.com

Atheneum Books
for Young Readers

TEEN.SimonandSchuster.com